THE FEARLESS CRUSADER

ONE MAN'S BATTLE AGAINST AN EVIL CORPORATION

SHRUTI PRIYAA

Srishti
Publishers & Distributors

Srishti Publishers & Distributors
A unit of AJR Publishing LLP
212A, Peacock Lane
Shahpur Jat, New Delhi – 110 049

editorial@srishtipublishers.com

First published by
Srishti Publishers & Distributors in 2024

10 9 8 7 6 5 4 3 2 1

This is a work of fiction. The characters, places, organisations and events described in this book are either a work of the author's imagination or have been used fictitiously. Any resemblance to people, living or dead, places, events, communities or organisations is purely coincidental.

Printed and bound in India.

Contents

ACKNOWLEDGEMENTS

I would like to extend my heartfelt gratitude to Lord Muruga for I'm nothing without him. I'm sure it was he who pulled me out of some really dark places and made me stronger and wiser. This book isn't possible without my trust and devotion to him.

I would like to share that this blast that happened in my village crushed the souls of many and there were few people who fought harder than Deva from this book. This book is dedicated to all of them.

My deepest thanks go to my family for their unwavering support and encouragement. Thanks for being proud of me and trusting me always!

I'm indebted to my dearest uncle, Sivakumar, who was the greatest inspiration for this story, and who, I know is showering his blessings upon me from up and above. Most of the incidents regarding the factory, the dates, and the details are inspired by his life before he left us. Wish you were here. I miss you.

I am especially grateful to Mr Natrajan, who guided me with his profound wisdom, deriving instances from his own experience when he fought the battle against the factory, with whom my uncle was crazy close. Your unwavering belief in my story instilled the courage I needed to share the truth.

To very few closest friends, thank you for your incredible patience and love and for being my sounding board as I recounted my experiences. Your trust in me when I had zero trust in myself surely made this possible. I'm indebted to you forever.

My publisher Arup, for pushing me to write more, motivating me beyond the limit, and taking my dream as his. My editor Stuti, for always staying my rock, and Alisha for her relentless support. I want to thank the entire team of Srishti for their undying trust in me.

Finally, to the readers, thank you for taking the time to engage with my story. It is my sincere hope that sharing my truth fosters an understanding of the painful events, enhances a connection between us, and perhaps even inspire you.

1
PROLOGUE
(The Annihilation)

1 December 2016
Achipatti village, Pollachi
Tamil Nadu

The velvety blackness of the sky is growing thick. The chirping of the crickets gets louder and more incessant with each passing second. The cacophony of these insects is actually music to the ears of the villagers of Achipatti because the chirping means that dusk has fallen and they can all snuggle up to sleep in their small, comfortable homes after a long, hard day in the fields. The men of the homes usually prefer to sleep out in the barn as it is cooler compared to their tiny abodes, and mostly because they prefer looking up at the peace-filled starry sky as they drift off into a deep slumber. Tonight's a full moon with clear skies, and the winter winds won't quit. The cows are making a racket at fervent intervals, making the villagers twist and turn in their sleep.

Head south in the village, and there's this narrow, creepy lane. During the day, it's still spooky, and even the toughest guys of the village feel a shiver down their spines and a rush of adrenaline when they have to take that route for work. The sides of the lane are filled with tall, scrappy greens. At the end of the lane is a huge, blue-coloured gate. Beyond that is a façade of what looks like a factory. It is a huge, high-standing concrete structure, and it looks out of place from the rest of the village as the premises are dry, lifeless, and forlorn.

'Veera Explosives', says the red board on one of the concrete structures. There is a hustle inside the building and a fiery red light blinks all of a sudden. The next moment, without warning, a roaring boom sends seismic waves throughout the premises and beyond. The indescribable sound of the explosion shoots up and hovers in the air as if it's meant to stay there, ripping it apart in the fraction of a second, reaching up and around with an unearthly, unstoppable force. The standing concrete structures are now fractured, the blocks of which are thrown far away from the premises. The ground is shaken by the impact of the blast and the vibration lasts for a couple of minutes, almost like an earthquake.

The chaos softens after a few minutes and the howls of the people around slowly start replacing the sound of the flare-up.

Inside the premises of the factory, beneath the debris of the fallen concrete blocks, is a fresh splash of blood… and a severed hand.

2
AT PERIL'S END

Present day

The prick of a splinter brings me back to my senses.

I have been standing in front of the old banyan tree, caressing its craggy trunk for, I haven't the faintest idea, how long. The ground is covered in dry algae, which imitates a fancy lawn. The luscious green shrubs all over seem to smile at me for some odd reason. The air is chilly and dampens my face. The happy rustle of leaves seems to soothe a dull ache inside me that I never knew existed, and finally the battered temple on the top with no walls, no gopuram, and no door; but is certainly the best temple I've ever been to—everything is nothing short of ecstasy!

The sort of ecstasy I have depended upon and enjoyed for too long; something which has given me solace since I was a little girl. And of course, years later, I'm here today hoping to find the same solace, but somehow, I feel everything except peace or succour. Numbing shades of anxiety, fear, anticipation, and panic creep upon me. Heaving a deep sigh as I press my palm harder on the bumps of the banyan tree, I hope this physical pain would somehow ease my pulsating heart.

I'm on the summit of a green hill in my native place named Achipatti, a small village in the town of Pollachi, which is located an hour away from Coimbatore in Tamil Nadu. Our village is known for its silent, lush beauty bordered by the stupendous green hills of the Western Ghats.

The bittersweet memories of the time I spent in this village are so fresh and seeped in with the rich flavour of the countryside. My entire childhood was physically intertwined with every inch of this place.

Every moment I spent here has breathed into me the rustic life which I have kept alive in every step of the way along my cosy city life. Whenever I think of the time I spent here, two things come to my mind.

One, the magnificently rugged yet humble beauty of the village.

And two, a man…

The man who was the embodiment of power, love, life and who utterly changed my life—especially after an incident that still sends shivers down my spine.

Tears emerge effortlessly and I blink them away. I look to my right at the jagged flight of stairs. I take them and hold the wall for support to prevent me from slipping on the algae. The bundle of papers in my hands keeps slipping, but I hold on to it tight as if it's my baby.

We used to call this hill 'mini Pachaimalai'—a miniature version of the infamous Pachaimalai hills on the stretch of Eastern Ghats. I smile. The name sounds funny to me now. I think of the reason why we named this hill that way. Well, we spent a lot of time in Pachaimalai hills when we trekked there years ago; and every time we climbed this small hill, it gave us the same feeling. It was kind of silly, but everything made absolute sense with him. Well, it *used* to.

I'm talking about the man who comes to my mind when I think of this village. My uncle, Deva.

My throat closes. It feels weird without him on this hill. I gaze at the shattered insides of the temple. The entry and the exit have no walls at all, and the exit leads straight to the edge of the hill. There is something melancholic, yet beautiful about destruction; and this temple is a living, well, *almost* living proof of that. Probably I find this ruptured exterior of the temple especially beautiful today because it resonates with my plight. The evening is falling and the breeze is getting chillier and heavier. I place the bundle of the case files at the foot of the broken idol as I collapse on my knees and pray.

The tears aren't far from spilling now. Tomorrow marks the reckoning. Two years of toiling under the hot sun, shedding blood, and working our fingers to the bone will finally meet its fate. But the thing is, the end of the day isn't something I can reckon or tame, though I badly want to. I've given it my all, and now I've handed the reins over to the Almighty. Come dawn, the verdict will be delivered, determining whether the years of ceaseless prayers and tears of this whole village will find comfort or face an irreparable harsh blow.

When you've done everything you could, everything humanly possible, there isn't much you can do except wait around for the answer. And worse, you have to be ready to handle both.

I step out of the temple and gaze down the hill. All it would take is a slip to put an end to the misery. But that would deny the whole purpose, wouldn't it?

The sun dips in the horizon and takes along with it the streaks of orange and out spurt the shades of brilliant navy blue into the sky. Whether you choose to call it God or nature, it doesn't matter. Looking at how that vast sky transforms in mere minutes makes you wonder, what are we in the grand scheme of things? We humans, we're a peculiar bunch. We strut around, thinking we've got it all figured out, but truth be told, we're just specks of dust in the mighty grip of the Creator. We dance about with pride, claiming control over everything, but in reality, what we know, what we think we know, is absolutely nothing.

God, or whatever force orchestrates the dance of millions of galaxies without a hitch, surely knows how to weave the tapestry of our lives. It's downright foolish for us to harbour such pride. We're nothing but the tiniest cogs in the vast machinery of His grand design. No matter how hard we strive to bend things to our will, we can't outsmart His grand plan. It's a humbling truth, reminding us that our role in this cosmic tale is minuscule at best. He determines everything...

And all I can do right now is surrender to Him.

Toward my right is a big boulder with a deep dent on top; it is used by the villagers as a diya during special occasions, and the whole village can see the diya. It's uncanny, but the villagers have always felt that the good is on its way every time they lay their eyes on the shimmering light up on the hill. The thick, dried wick is still there and the depression is devoid of oil. I head back into the temple, grab the pot of oil near the idol and empty that into the dent. There isn't any matchbox nearby.

Damn it, I think. *Not today.*

I need to find the matchbox. I have to light the lamp for the whole village to believe that we would finally win. Even if not, I want them all to sleep peacefully tonight, placing their trust and hope in the gleam of the flame.

"Looking for this, Shravya?" I hear a manly voice behind me and my heart leaps to my mouth.

"Hey!" I turn around to see the handsome man in his late twenties with a matchbox in his extended hand. It is Aadhi. My breath quivers. He is six foot tall, has a great physique and he's someone who would go to any length for me. His ruggedness, bearded face, deep yet feminine eyes and thin lips that pucker in excitement at the sight of me, always make my heart skip a beat. He told me two years back that he was in love with me. But I didn't have the courage to tell him I felt the same way, and eventually let myself get distracted with more important things.

"Light it," he says and steps towards me. He then looks at the horizon. "Let them sleep peacefully tonight."

"Can you light it with me?" I ask, and immediately regret the question. Doing such an important act together is, in a way, the peak of intimacy and I do not want it right now. But it is too late as he is here towering over me, his gaze soft. He hands the matchbox to me. I light the match and look at him. He brings his hand towards mine and together we light the lamp of hope.

A tear escapes my eye and he wipes it before it falls on the ground.

"Hey, we have come this far. And we have faced it all," he says. "We'll definitely face whatever comes next."

I nod.

We sit on the big boulder near the lamp that marks the edge of the hill and overlooks the entire village and two others nearby. I can see my uncle's farm from here. The lights are off unlike those days when it used to stay lit up like a Christmas tree. People used to gather and hang out at his farm and gaze at the stars above. His farm used to be the epitome of happiness and now it is forlorn and pitch black—darker than the falling night.

"Shravya ..." Aadhi says, nudging my face away from the direction of my uncle's farm. "There were good times. Don't let all of it go just because of *that* incident."

Good times, the word repeats itself inside my head. *Good times.*

Aadhi's right. There were many... and those make up most of my memory. Wonder why I hadn't reminisced about any of them till now.

3
GOOD TIMES

14 January 2016
Coimbatore

I could feel the heat gently warming up my skin through the glass windows, and strangely, it felt good. The smile grew on my face. I twisted and turned and snuggled a bit more into the bed, letting out a slight moan. Nothing beats the sleep that shoves its way from within you after the sun is up. I was at my parents' house in Coimbatore. Such a peaceful city. Tolerable hubbub, manageable extravaganza, sensible crowd, delicious food and most importantly, wondrous weather with the Western Ghats harbouring it like a majestic mamma. This city is terribly underrated, in fact. But it's a good thing because all the glorified cities are flocked by people from all over and soon enough, the nestled, intricate beauty that only a few can relish, falls right through.

"Shravya!" I heard my mother's voice booming across the room. "We have to leave in an hour. Wake up! It's past ten."

"Five more minutes," I said. And nothing beats this extra five minutes of sleep.

"I know how long your five minutes are!" She stood in the doorway, fully dressed. She was wearing a brown-coloured cotton salwar kameez which looked crisp and neatly pressed. I have no idea how she looked chic and stylish and, more importantly, fresh all the time. As if she had just come out of the laundry.

"Oh, come on!" I squirmed. "Why do we have to leave this early? Pongal isn't even until tomorrow. Why can't we go then?"

"You know why!"

I rubbed my eyes vigorously as I tried adjusting them to the morning blue. "Yeah mom," I said, sarcasm unfurling from my mouth just like the drool. "This is the face of the person that knows," I point to my swollen, sleepy face.

"Right," my mom smiled and sat beside me on the bed. "Deva is returning to the village today from his solo trip to Rameshwaram."

I instantly sat up straight on the bed, my eyes wide open. The sheets were thrown aside and I literally jumped up as if a sudden spurt of adrenaline had been pumped through my body. The blur was gone and my heart was racing.

"Now that's the face of the person who knows," my mom laughed. "Sleep, Shravya. You're welcome to take the five minutes you told me about."

"Mom!" I laughed and threw a pillow at her. "You're serious though? He's coming back today?"

"I am. Your father just got a text from him."

"Wow!" I jumped down from the bed. "Today's gonna be so much fun!"

"Yeah. And the text also mentioned that he's brought you the tickets for some recent stupid movie that you like?"

"Really? He's the best!"

My mother sighed and walked out of the room. "I will never understand your relationship with that man! He treats you better than his own child and you, the sleepy head that you are, prefer to throw up the sheets high in the air at the mention of his name."

I laughed, glad my mom was in a good mood today.

"You better make the bed before you get ready!"

And there it went. I sighed. *Just when I thought I could get away!*

* * *

The car ride from Coimbatore to Pollachi and then to our hometown Achipatti was always the best. My sister Shriya sat beside me, all dressed up. She's six years younger to me but is way more mature. She is just nine years old but she had paired a cute ochre sleeveless top and a short skirt, her hair neatly in place and I wore a gaudy-pink short kurti and shabby red coloured pants, my hair just clipped back.

"Your pants suck," she said.

"Why?"

"It is red for god's sake!"

"So?"

"Who wears it with baby pink? Only a dork."

"Fine," I said and pinched her thigh. She yelped in pain. I grinned at her. Served her right.

"You!" she pulled my hair like a maniac and I screamed in agony.

"Girls!" my mom yelled from the front seat. "Stop it right now or we'll make you two dorks get down and go without you. Especially you, Shravya!"

"Why especially me? She started it!"

"Why don't you dress up properly at least once as she says?" my mom turned to look at me. "Why do you always pick outfits like some homeless person who seems to have suddenly found clothes and decides to wear the first one they lay their eyes on?"

"What?" I asked. "Seriously! What? That doesn't even make sense. Why do you always have a problem with everything I do? Why can't I just be me? Why should I be perfect like you two fashion gurus?"

"Oh, you stop that now!" my mom said.

"Let her be," my dad spoke for the first time. We had crossed the city and were now on the scenic route to Pollachi. The car's vibe had calmed down just like the vibe outside. My sister put her head out of the window and was peacefully gazing at the abundant beauty along the road. My dad and I were enjoying our favourite Tamil songs blasting through the roof and my mom had plugged in her earplugs and was fast asleep.

We are headed to my dad's younger brother's house in Achipatti. He is a man of honour with three kids and a loving wife. His name is Rudran, and he is definitely my most favourite uncle among my relatives. There is also someone who means a lot more to me than any of my relatives; someone whom I consider a part of my family, well, certainly a part of my life—my uncle's best friend, uncle Deva.

As Achipatti is my native village, we come here during every festival and sometimes, we just drive up there for no reason at all because we have the best time here. My uncle Rudran always welcomes us with open arms. My dad and uncle Rudran share a special bond since childhood. Rudran uncle was the youngest and my dad the eldest of four brothers. The two middle brothers were settled in different states and they rarely visited us. As my dad and Rudran uncle lived close by, which was intentional, we made it a point to visit their place whenever we found a reason, and most of the times when we hadn't found one!

Rudran uncle's place was a typical Chettinad house—one with a vast courtyard and spacious rooms embellished with marbles and teak. The airy interiors, the polished mahogany beds, the open roof above the courtyard, the ample front and backyards, the well-fed cows and poultry, the rose garden in the front—everything about the house would make you forget all your worries and fill you with gratitude for life. That's what a trip to a village would do to you.

Rudran uncle was actually a landlord with several acres of land in his name. However, it was not only the land and money that had won him respect. It was his dedication and the way he treated people that had earned him the success and the fortune he enjoyed.

Several years back, when I was seven years old, we had gone to the village for Pongal. That night a gentleman had come to Rudran uncle's home for dinner. On seeing him, my uncle had almost tripped while trying to run and hug him. I had never seen my uncle react that way except for when he saw my dad. That man wore a loose pair of denim pants and a black shirt unbuttoned till his chest. He was a tall, majestic man with a dark complexion, bright smile, deep eyes and ruffled hair. He had a noticeable scar on his left temple. Basically, an extremely good looking, rugged man who did not look his age. My dad went and greeted him with an ample hug and so did uncle Rudran. I wondered who that man was.

Soon I learned that he was my uncle Rudran's childhood friend and his name was Deva, and that the two were close like brothers. He hailed from Achipatti village, but had evolved as a protector, a harbourer and a go-to person for all the villagers when things went south.

The moment uncle Deva stepped inside the house, a group of villagers with sullen faces came bowing down at the entrance. Uncle Deva and uncle Rudran received them and they all sat in the courtyard in a deep discussion. I hid behind one of the massive pillars on the edge of the courtyard and I could pick out some words like 'Veera Explosives', 'money', 'land' and some man called 'Manivannan' and his family... something about them missing. It was a pretty serious discussion. I didn't grab the details of it, but uncle Deva's face was sullen, his head hung low the whole while as if he was going to break down. I also heard them talk about water pollution and cattle dying because of it. As the discussion proceeded, I saw uncle Deva getting furious and make a few phone calls. Soon enough, the villagers left with happy faces.

My mom then told me that uncle Deva had just called up the area councillor who had sided with the bad guys, and that the councillor had apologized. I didn't want to ask any further as I was bored by then.

"How did he scare a politician? That too on call?" I asked.

"Ah, that's just his reputation," my mom said. "There isn't one soul in this vicinity who isn't afraid of Deva. He's the godfather of the people around here. They idolize him and trust him with all their hearts. Do you know why Rudran loves him? It's because Deva saved his life when he was young. Rudran was about to meet with an accident at the entrance of his school when Deva pushed him off the road right on time and got hurt pretty badly in turn. He was hospitalized for a month."

The more I heard about him, the more I realized this man was a folklore hero—straight from the Rudyard Kipling books. Obviously, I developed a great sense of admiration for him as my whole family treated him with so much love and respect. Well, not just my family. The entire village. I saw a lot of people come along and ask for his help—old men, couples, politicians, groups of villagers—all sorts of people despite their clan and class. All I noticed was that this man treated everyone the same; with utmost respect and humility.

I patiently waited my turn for him to notice me just the way he had noticed the other people. Finally, after every villager had left the house, he had the time to address me.

"Hey kiddo," he said with an ardent smile, I responded happily and respectfully, making sure I made a good impression. He spoke to me just like he spoke to my parents. He never treated me like I was some immature kid or looked down upon me. I loved that and I loved him; not because I knew he was a hero, but because he treated me beautifully. He instantly made plans with me to take me to the well on his farm the next day and teach me swimming. I readily agreed. When he was about to leave, he carried me on top of his shoulders and swirled me which made me laugh like I never had.

The next day was something I recall every day and it has remained a sweet memory till date. He tied me with one of those palm thingies that float on water. These palm floats were the countryside version of water tubes.

"This looks funny," I said. "Like I'm pregnant," I patted the hollow palm float.

Uncle Deva smiled at me and pushed me into the well. I was out of air. Terrified, I swam. Yeah, just like that! I just swam because there was nothing else I could do.

I learnt that day that the best way to face your worst fear was to stand in front of it, face it and politely ask it to shove it up its ass.

Deva uncle, I called him. And since then he has been an integral part of my life. I dialled him up when things went horribly wrong or during the teeniest of discomforts; and that man, well, he was just there for me. In the way I wanted. As a friend, a father, a moral support, a shoulder to lean on, and most importantly, as the only person who expected nothing from me and who never judged me. He became a part of our extended family.

Deva uncle also had acres of land like Rudran uncle, but he had sold most of it at low prices to the people in need. He travelled around to help people—saving them from mental and physical turmoil. He had won a lot of bravery awards for saving the lives of accident victims. He had also built small shelters for street dogs and gave them up for adoption. But the worst pain always follows the best people. His wife had passed away in an accident when their only son was five, whom I'd never met. Uncle Deva did not remarry.

Probably the pain from that tragedy had urged him to make others' lives a little better. Six months back, he had been to Rameshwaram to help a group of cancer-stricken children who needed urgent money for treatment. He had taken care of the entire expenditure and stayed until the procedure was over. Though many kids had terminal cancer, he did his best to save them. I knew that experience would have been pretty heavy for him emotionally, and I was carefully planning to cheer him up today.

I heaved a sigh as I hung out my head out the window. I should give him a big hug first and make it a point to never ask him about the kids from Rameshwaram, or let anyone else throw idiotic questions like "how was your trip?"

Within an hour, I would be seeing him after three whole months. My excitement knew no bounds when my dad took the final turn into the vast front yard of Rudran uncle's house. I could see my two uncles laughing and catching up with a large plate of groundnuts, sweets, *chev* and tender coconuts sitting on the raised platform around the house called the *thinnai*. Typical of them. Soon enough, they saw our car and both of them almost sprinted to receive us. Deva uncle's eyes darted around quickly in search of me and the moment he saw me, he reached out and tried to lift me high, but failed miserably. As usual, he wore a dark coloured shirt and jeans.

"My! You've grown a lot my little girl!" he said, all smiles.

"Deva uncle!" I said and hugged him tight. "How are you?"

"I'm good, my princess. How have you been?" his baritone voice was now high pitched with excitement.

"I'm good. I just missed you."

"So did I, my girl!" he patted my head and I could see him choking up a bit.

"Deva! My sweet brother from another mother!" my mom called out to him. And pointing to me, she said, "She is your problem now. I have disowned her."

"Hi *Anni!*" Deva uncle bowed before my mom. The word anni meant brother's wife. "I would love to adopt this child any day any time!" he said. "She's just perfect."

"Duh," Shriya said as she passed by us. "Try looking at her clothes before you decide!"

Deva uncle looked at me and laughed. "Good choice, my princess," he said. "I love your pants!"

"Couple of dorks," my sister mumbled and left. She did not connect emotionally with people easily, and though both Rudran and Deva uncle tried to bond with her, she always gave them the cold shoulder. They loved me as I was more of a kid than her. Though younger, she was mature, one with the attitude, confident and wouldn't give a rat's ass about anything. I was naïve, excited about the little things, vulnerable, loving and innocent about the ways of the world—no wonder the uncles picked me.

Soon enough, we were making Pongal arrangements. Well, they were making it. Uncle Deva and I, as usual, headed to the well on his farm. The weather wasn't very pleasant as we expected. The sun soared high up, blinding the skies and the eyes, the heat travelling its way up our bodies. The thought of a dip in the well certainly seemed more exciting by the second. The water had gone down a few feet as compared to the last time. I looked at Deva uncle and he gave me one of his signature smiles. I didn't think twice. I jumped in with my clothes. The water was so refreshing and cool, like the first taste of an ice cube after a spicy dinner. In an instant, I felt alive. My uncle sat on the edge of the well, cheering me up as I swam like a pro.

"You've gotten so much better, sweetie," he said.

"I had the best teacher in the world," I said as I did the backstroke efficiently. "What do you expect?"

"Don't make me blush," my uncle said and laughed. "Hey, by the way, I didn't tell you. My son is back from boarding school. He will be joining us for Mattu Pongal day after tomorrow."

Suddenly, I felt a mixture of anger and insecurity surging up and I let it pass by swimming away from him, in the other direction. I was upset I wouldn't get his attention any more.

"Great," I said.

"Woah, woah, what's with your face?"

"What do you mean?"

"That stare, that cute snort, that sulk and don't even get me started on the angry balling of your fists and swimming away from me!"

I stayed silent.

"Oh my god, you're jealous!" he laughed. "Of my son!"

"Oh please," I snapped. "No way."

"Okay, your call. But let me tell you this. For starters, he is five years older than you. There is something else you should know about him," he paused and looked away, "he is a gem. He's perfect, unlike me."

"Oh, come on, you're perfect."

"I rarely am. You know his mom passed away when he was very young," his voice broke and he spoke again. "Thing is, she passed away on his birthday. She had been to her mom's place in Coimbatore and was returning to celebrate his birthday. A drunk lorry driver drove her off the road and she died on the spot." He bowed his head and I knew he was holding back his guttural sobs. My stomach twisted. I had no idea what to do as my heartbeat shot up. He continued talking after what seemed like an eternity.

"We couldn't celebrate his birthday ever because all I do every year is drink away my sorrows and he would be left alone to do his homework. I wasn't around much when he was growing up as, you know, I ran around to help those who I thought needed me; but I forgot the only one who actually needed me. Even now, look at me. I'm bonding beautifully with you while I have never given this kind of attention to my son even for a day," he looked up and wiped his tears. "But that kid never hated me for it. He grew to be this wonderful, understanding person—so matured, that he always took care of himself and me. He understood me and sympathized with me instead of being cross that I had never spent time with him like a normal dad." Uncle Deva smiled. "My son should be the last person you should be jealous of, because, you know, there are tons of reasons why he should be jealous of you. I might be an amazing person to everyone, but I forgot how to be a good dad."

I teared up. I never expected this. I just wanted to get out of the water and hug him and tell him that he was an amazing dad, but I just drifted in the water, my heart warming up to his son whom I'd never met.

"Come on now!" I smiled at my uncle. I really didn't know what to say. I was just fifteen years old and I had no idea how to console a man who was my father's age. "Cheer up!" I said. "You're going to meet him soon!"

"Oh yeah . . . I am," he said, trying hard to fake a smile.

"So, from day after tomorrow, your trophy kid gets the main stage and I would be sidelined."

Deva uncle's eyes widened for a second and then he burst into laughter. Thank god, finally, one of my dumb ideas had actually worked.

"No way, Shravya!" he said, wiping the grin off his face. "You'd always be the main one," he winked. "At least for me."

"Aww, I know. I'm excited to meet your son though. Really."

"I'm damn sure you'd love him!" he grinned again.

"Sure, but not as much as I love you, uncle Deva."

"Really?"

"Yes. You'd always be the main one," I said as I plunged into the water, came back out and winked at him. "At least for me."

4
THE PRICE OF INNOCENCE
Archana

7 October 2006 – TEN YEARS AGO

People think it's a boon to be born intelligent. Is it, though? The day I was born, which was on 3 October 1983, some astrologer had predicted that I was going to make it big as an intellectual.

I still don't know how he predicted that. He had said that my Guru and Ketu had aligned in a single box that determined my intellect and that Venus was at peak in my *Jaathagam*. Sounded complicated, so yeah, it had to be true.

Ever since, or at least I hoped it was because of that, no one reacted big when I wanted to leave my village to go study in a big city or when I got straight A's in my school or when I won every single inter and intra school competition. My parents rarely visited me in Chennai where I studied in a matric school, staying in a hostel. Hell, my parents did not even come for my college counselling. Do you know why? Being traditional villagers, they had this urge to get the validation of the small society that operated within the village. Having a kid like me who was way too educated was a threat to the village society because they were all illiterate and preferred to be that way. I was different; I did not behave the way they expected girls to behave—dress up, show up, cook and be respectful. I did not dress up, did not show up as I preferred to be in my room, my nose into my book, and I detested people too much to be respectful. So, in places where my parents should have been proud of me, they felt humiliated.

However, as prodigal as I was as a student, I lacked social skills. Being around people made me nauseous and I felt intimidated. I couldn't even ask someone what the time was without stammering and stuttering; it made me self-dependent, rather than independent.

Can't find the difference? For independence, you need to have good people skills. You go out, meet people (sometimes bring them home), show them who you are and make heads turn as you walk.

But by self-dependence, what I mean is, you just shut out people, live in a box, do your work and survive, without depending on anyone. There's a difference. Independence is based on confidence, while self-dependence is based on fear. And also, for independence, you *kind of* need people to recognize that you *are* independent. But for self-dependence, for starters, nobody cares about you and that is the beauty of it.

Oops. I haven't introduced myself yet. Sorry, I'm a bit talkative and I usually go off track. Ironic considering I lack social skills, is it? Well, the truth is, that was a long, long time ago. I have changed now—changed to become quite the opposite. We all do, don't we? We all have the tendency to change into something that we never thought we would be. *Especially* into something we never thought of. You won't believe the stream of education I chose to pursue. Law!

The one field that required you to be around, earn from, suck the blood out of, breathe life into—*people*. My story would make you believe that we become what we hate. Some books say that we are actually spiritually affined to the things that we love or hate, and life certainly brings you to it. See? Again, I went off track. Don't blame me. I'm a lawyer! We are paid to do that.

My name is Archana. I was born in Achipatti, a beautiful village near Pollachi. I was the only child to my parents. My dad was a farmer and my mom, a homemaker. We lived a happy life in a small cottage. As you might have guessed, our village was known to be fertile. So breathtaking. So peaceful. Hence, lack of opportunities for someone like me. It might sound cliche, but as the astrologer had put it, books had been my best friends. And there weren't enough of them in the village. That's why I preferred the big cities. I don't want to deny it and it pains me to say that I looked down upon the village—not its fertility, but the simple minds of people. I detested lack of intelligence. If there was one thing I couldn't tolerate, it was ignorance that came along with judgement. They judged me for being different, loathed me for breaking the glass ceiling and after I graduated from a reputed law college, they invited me back with respect. Duh, people!

Probably that was the reason why I hated visiting the village even during holidays or festivals. Though my parents had every reason to gloat about me after my graduation, they still read the faces of the people they considered as the society. When the village finally decided to celebrate me, they did too!

I had to come back to Achipatti after graduation. Just for a month, I decided, before I could apply for masters. I needed a break. The village seemed eerily familiar except for the under-construction building complex of some factory.

Good! Finally, some technological development.

I had finished reading all five John Grisham novels I had brought over in two weeks. Man, I love courtroom dramas. Chills! Having nothing else to do, I decided to take a walk around the factory area to see how the construction was coming along. The humble beauty of the village was intoxicating. I smiled as I rubbed the goosebumps off emerging from the chill in the air. I wore a yellow kurti and a pair of jeans that day, my hair flowing freely. I think it would be a bit boastful, but it's the truth. I'm beautiful. It takes real confidence to say that! But I did not know until I had so many people telling me that constantly. I'd heard 'Woah, you're pretty' a hell lot more than 'Woah, you're smart' though I craved for the latter. During college, many guys proposed but I was interested in none. Truth is, the very concept of falling in love, sex, marriage was pointless to me.

Until that day. I had no idea that day was about to change my life.

I was walking in the direction of the building when I saw a lane in front of me—a lot greener, darker and uncannily chillier than the rest of the village. The hairs on my neck stood up.

"What are you doing here?" I heard a sudden, deep voice from behind me and I jumped out of my skin. I turned around to see a tall, bearded man in a soiled T-shirt and a questionable pair of pants. He looked to be in his thirties, definitely a decade older than me, at least. I don't know how to put it, but my breath got caught in my throat the moment I laid eyes on him. The chills increased still as I slowly looked at his face, taking in all the details. Never once in my life had I ever wanted to check out a man's face. I had never felt attracted to even the most handsome ones. But the sight of this man sent a jolt through my body.

His eyes were deep, his complexion dark and sexy and the way he glared at me in anger gave me a tingle in between my legs—a feeling I'd heard my friends talk about constantly, but never felt. His beard was so thick that I could hardly make out his lips. The fact that I was trying to get a peek at a guy's lips for the first time ever, made me blush. He had a scar on his left temple and had a perfectly-shaped nose. Such sharp features. Insanely handsome. Who was he?

"Hello! You deaf?" He spoke again, waving his hand in front of my face. He seemed to be getting angrier by the minute. His forehead was creased. I smiled and I saw him taking in my face, just for a second. The creases faded and he looked away. Yep, the effect I had on boys! Didn't realize I could have that on a man too!

"Hey," I spoke.

"What are you doing here?" He looked at me again, this time, his anger receding.

"I came to see the factory."

"You're not allowed here."

"Says who?"

He glared at me. I smiled. It wasn't intentional, but it just came. He looked away. Good, more smiling required.

"This place isn't safe. Go back."

"Hello, I was born here. Who are you to say that?"

"Born here?" he squirmed. "What's your name?"

I wanted to stall him, toy with him, invoke his anger and in turn invoke those girly feels again. But I wanted to relish it slowly, not all at one go.

"I'm Archana," I said.

He looked thoughtful. "Manivannan anna's daughter?" he asked.

"Yes."

A smile emerged. I was weak in the knees. His anger made me weak but his smile made me weaker. Damn!

"How are you, kid?"

Kid?

"Kid?"

"Yeah, I heard you were in college."

"I graduated."

"Good. Good."

"Anyway, I need to visit the factory, if you don't mind." I was pissed at him for calling me a kid and it was obvious, maybe to him too. But for some reason he decided to overlook that. Maybe he was married. I turned stiff and sullen. Jealousy—an emotion I had rarely felt apart from that evoked by my academic nemesis.

"I'll join you," he said, "I'm headed there myself."

"Okay."

We walked through the dark lane. The chills were back. But somehow, with this handsome stranger beside me, I did not mind.

"Who are you, by the way?" I asked.

He smiled at me. My nerves tightened. "My name is Deva," he said.

5
PONGAL DAYS

15 January 2016
Achipatti

The first day of Pongal—Bhogi—was over. We do not do much on this day. We do not follow the custom of throwing away our old things into fire. Rather, we just sit on the thinnai and eat up our sugarcanes and litter the ground with the chewed remains. We also go to Rudran uncle's farm and enjoy the tasty treat that he serves for the entire village—the tradition he values only second after honouring his cows on Mattu Pongal.

Today was the second day of Pongal, also known as Surya Pongal—the day we offer our prayers to the Sun god and thank him for the ample harvest that year. The entrances of houses are adorned with *maayilai thoranam*—beautiful hangings made from mango leaves. We dressed up nicely and headed with all the things required to make Pongal, to my dad's farm. That's how it was—Surya Pongal at my dad's farm and Mattu Pongal at Rudran uncle's. The day passed by quickly and pleasantly. In the evening, we visited Rudran uncle's farm and tied sugarcanes to trees, forming an arch and we served Pongal on banana leaf along with banana, with incense sticks pierced on it. We walked barefoot to every nook and corner of the fields, praying for more harvest that year. We polished away the rest of the Pongal for dinner, and dozed off on the terrace.

The next morning we had tons of things to do. All my cousins and most of my pesky relatives had arrived at uncle Rudran's house and as usual, I woke up late, got a good thrashing from mom and started my day. For some reason, I was looking forward to meet Deva uncle's son, just to see how he looked, how he spoke, how he dressed and if he had the same qualities as his dad.

Though Deva uncle had helped a lot of people, he hardly appreciated anyone. That monologue about his son certainly invoked my curiosity and twirled it around to an extent that it metamorphosed into an inexplicable urge to lay my eyes on him. I didn't know if it was girly instincts or mere excitement, but I made it a point to take suggestions from my mean little sister on how to dress up for the day.

She convinced me to wear a cream coloured anarkali with a doodle of blue and red on the chest area.

"Wow this really accentuates my boobs," I said to my sister.

"The whole purpose of an anarkali, dear girl," my sister said as she did my hair, standing on top of a small stool to match my height.

"No. I feel conscious."

She turned my chin towards her. "You're dressing up for a guy, aren't you?"

"What?" I rolled my eyes and puckered my mouth in shock. "What?"

"Repetition," she said. "Sign of guilt."

"How old are you, if I may ask?"

"Come on, girl. This is the first time in years that you've wanted to look good. It's kinda obvious."

"Really?"

"Yeah, pathetic even."

"Oh stop."

"Who's the guy?" she asked, stepping down from the stool and picking up her makeup.

"Don't put stuff on my face." I pushed her away.

"Allow me, missy," she said. "For once I want to see how you'd look had you been properly tamed. Anyway, answer me. Who are you dressing up for?"

"It's no one. I don't even know him."

"So there is a 'him'. Good."

I repeated the episode with Deva uncle to my sister.

"Wow, that's intriguing," she said. "Deva uncle himself is darn handsome. I'm sure his son would also be a looker."

"That's weird. Don't objectify Deva uncle." I look at her in disgust.

"I'm just being practical. Deva uncle is handsome as hell…but what if his wife is…I mean was not?" she said.

"Oh, shut it, you mean little piece of…"

"Wait. Look," she pointed to the mirror.

In place of an oily-faced, unkempt person that I always saw, I was gazing at a beautiful teenager with a beautiful face and a complicated hairstyle that complimented my features. I couldn't believe my eyes.

"Have I been this pretty all this time?" I asked.

My sister walked away from me with a sigh and I was pretty sure she mumbled something when she slammed the door.

I was sure I drew the awed eyes of my relatives, but I pretended I hadn't noticed. When Deva uncle saw me, he burst into laughter and so did everyone around me, including my parents.

"What's this for, young lady?" he asked.

Everyone pointed and laughed. I guess they were used to my homeless looks and this was too much for them to take. I was deeply embarrassed. I ran out of words and I literally ran out of the house into the front yard, stepping on the beautiful *kolams*—the rangoli designs that my aunt and the women of the house had drawn using rice flour.

"Watch out, Shravya!" a relative yelled and I turned around to look who it was. Big mistake. I didn't notice the raised platform in front of the house, tripped on it and fell flat on the ground. The chickens scampered about, a cow mooed in fear and two dogs barked in terror. I rubbed the mud off my face along with the makeup, and in front of me I saw a car stop and out came a tall, handsome boy who had a face almost like uncle Deva.

* * *

"Ah, let it go. Things happen," Deva uncle said as we sat at the edge of Rudran uncle's farm, eating sweet Pongal. For every Pongal we headed out to uncle Rudran's farm and the women of the house cooked the Pongal in two huge pots—one the sweet Pongal, and the other, the white Pongal, also called the *ven* Pongal, which I was crazy about. It tasted phenomenal with the spicy *thogayal*—a mixture of mint, coriander, coconuts, red chillies and a lot of other ingredients—which my grandmother made. That day was Mattu Pongal—the third day of Pongal and that was the most fun one in our village.

In some time, we had to bathe our cows, goats and dogs and we had to apply colour on their bodies. My younger cousins were having a lot of fun in the well, splashing about, without worrying about anything.

It had been a rude awakening for me. The moment I felt the embarrassment hitting me hard as I fell, I knew I was no longer a child. And that was pretty hard to take. Only Deva uncle came to my rescue. He picked me up from the ground and gave his famous stare to the laughing relatives who quieted down immediately. He then took me out to uncle Rudran's farm for the big talk. After a while, everyone started coming to the farm to cook Pongal, and in the midst of work, they had forgotten about my epic fall. We sat behind a big banyan tree that pretty much hid me from everyone. I had basically absconded because of the embarrassment.

"I wanted to make an impression," I confessed, "in front of your son."

"I figured," Uncle Deva said and smiled.

"How?" I asked him, my eyes wide.

"It's obvious. I think I know you well enough to know what you like."

I shrugged. "But I failed."

"Happens." He nodded understandingly.

I looked at him, surprised, "You know I'm talking about your own son, right?"

"Yeah, so?"

"How can you be supportive even now?"

"Because you're my baby girl, Shravya," he said and playfully punched my arm. "You're literally my daughter. When would you ever get that?" his eyes had turned glassy again and it pained me. I wondered how the ever-angry, powerful folklore hero could turn teary so effortlessly. That tinge of vulnerability in him made him more beautiful.

"I do now," I said and my voice choked.

"And my son would be lucky to have you," he said and I punched his arm.

Dusk had fallen and all the clean animals, their bodies painted with colour, were now ready to take their shabby step on the carefully carved dung decorated with herbs and fire. That was the tradition. This is just to clean their hooves as they tend to get worm infested in winter. Even the teeniest thing we address today as tradition has science behind it. Pity we don't know it.

Every time the animal took a step, we all yelled "Pongalo Pongal" at the top of our voices. Just when a calf took its step and I was about to yell, I stopped short.

"Hey," I heard a deep voice next to me. It was uncle Deva's son. My breath got caught in my throat and I swallowed.

"Hey," I said and took my time to look at him clearly for the first time. I had just had a glimpse of him that proved he was uncle Deva's son when I had fallen. Nothing more. But only now did I notice his deep, feminine eyes, creased forehead, thick hair, wheatish skin, bearded face and the fact that he was six-feet tall. God, this guy looked dreamy.

"I met all of your cousins," he said, his voice deep. "Except you. You disappeared after I saw you."

"You can imagine why," I said. "I was embarrassed."

"Of what exactly?" he asked.

"You know... I fell down."

"So what? It happens."

Like father, like son, I thought, rubbing off my goosebumps.

"It was embarrassing." I asserted.

"I wouldn't worry about that. Well, you are literally the prettiest girl I've seen around here," he said. "You better be embarrassed about that if you really want something to be embarrassed about."

My heart skipped a beat. *What the heck?* He did not just say that! Uncle Deva had certainly missed telling me his son was this forthcoming about his thoughts.

"Sorry if I made you uncomfortable," he said.

"No... no," I said and adjusted my hair. "No."

"Okay," he smiled.

"I'm Shravya," I said and held my arm out.

"Nice to meet you, Shravya," he paused and looked deep into my eyes. "I'm Aadhi," he said and smiled. I froze.

I still remember that smile—the best one I'd ever seen. Sweet, sexy and manly... a deadly combination which made me weak in the knees for the first time.

That instant I knew this guy was trouble.

* * *

6
LOVE IS IN THE DUSTY AIR

Archana

7 October 2006 – TEN YEARS AGO

Achipatti Village

We did not speak a word as we walked through the chilly lane. I was pissed at him for calling me a kid, and somehow, he seemed quieter than me. Was it because of my presence? Nah. I knew it was something more than that because his face stiffened with each step ahead. The tall, overgrown shrubs on our sides seemed to be attacking me. I moved closer to him holding my arms tight, as if hugging myself.

"It will pass," he said. "Just a few hundred metres."

His voice brought back the tingles and a shot of adrenaline rushed through. What on earth were these feelings?

"Are you associated with the factory people?"

He guffawed.

"Quite the opposite."

"Meaning?"

"I'm waging a war against them," he said, his face stiff. "To make them leave."

"What?"

"They are parasites. Liars. Blood suckers."

The creases were back and I could hardly listen to what he said.

"These factory guys?"

"Yep. They are here for the water. They pretended to buy this fertile land for plantation and started building a frigging explosives factory!

You know what it's going to do to the village? It's going to turn it into a graveyard."

"Woah! That's a tad unbelievable."

"Our fertility is only because of the water. The waste from this factory will turn it into poison. I have got to stop the construction."

I stayed silent. Our pace got slower.

"And how are you going to do that?"

It was his turn to be quiet. I heard a little sigh.

"No idea. Every day I head up here, make a scene, yell at them, throw curse words and come back. I tried reaching out to the police so many times. But they are untouchable."

"That's bad," I said. My concentration was no longer on his pretty face. Fighting with a corporation. That's why his T-shirt was soiled with cement. He had been going to the construction site too often. A surge of warmth filled me.

He shook his head as if coming out of an absorbing thought and said, "Anyway, I have no idea why I told you all this. Don't take this to your head, kid."

"Stop calling me that," I blurted.

Though I expected a 'why' or a shocked reaction from him, he just turned quiet, the creases on his forehead long gone. Probably it was too obvious that I was drawn to him, and for some reason, he didn't want to address it.

The cement-dust filled air in front of us told me we had reached the construction site.

"So, what do we do now?" I asked.

"We?" he laughed. "I go there, fight with them, burn their butts. You can watch the construction, talk to those pretentious, english-speaking muttonheads, and do a case study. I'm sure they would entertain that."

I couldn't help but smile.

I was drawn to his appearance. Now it was more than that.

"I don't think I'll do that," I said.

"Really?" he raised his brows.

"Yeah. English-speaking muttonheads are not my type anyway."

That invoked a big smile on his pretty face, and he looked down, making sure I did not catch him smiling. I did.

"Are you married?" I said.

Yep, that's right. I asked what I asked. Straightaway. His face changed in a fraction of a second. Damn, I knew I had touched the wrong pie. In his language, burnt the wrong butt.

"I was," he said. No surprise there. He looked older. Thirties definitely.

"Divorced?" I asked.

"Widowed," he swallowed. My knees buckled.

"I'm sorry."

"Thank you," he said. After a pause, he had another question.

"How old are you?"

"Twenty-three."

He smiled.

"Kid."

"Stop that," I pushed his arm. He retrieved it immediately, gasping a tad as if my hand was made of fire. He moved away from me for a second, heaved a sigh and then moved back close. Probably because I was afraid of the chills.

A gentleman, I thought.

"Old man!" I said out loud. He smiled and quickly controlled it.

"I am."

"How old?"

"Older than your dad."

"Very funny."

He nodded and walked along. A group of people were carrying out the construction amidst the smoke of cement. In the middle stood a tall, good-looking young man, speaking animatedly with large hand gestures with someone who looked like the engineer in charge. I looked at Deva. The creases were back. His breaths turned shallow.

"Vijay Kumar," he said and I looked back again at the handsome man inside the cloud of cement. "He is the reason for everything. Evil being. Wish I could get my hands on that b—"

With that, he walked fast with fury, almost sprinted inside the cloud and got into a loud argument with Vijay. But Vijay had a strange reaction to this. He just smiled sarcastically, guffawed a little and spoke in a calming manner while Deva fired out his guts. I knew in an instant that Vijay was a dangerous being. You can trust the one filled with anger, filled with pain, one who always has a cross face, but you can never ever trust a calm person. If they can go through turmoil and anger and do not let it show on their face, trust me, they are capable of anything.

The world always judges the one with the cross, angry face. But I knew better. And for some reason, I wanted that calm smile on his face to crack.

There was a loud tussle and the workers pulled Deva away. As expected, Vijay still stayed calm. Some would have even found him attractive, you know? He was the rich, chocolate, yet bad boy kind—the kind kids fall in love with. The kids who wouldn't know when the sweet mask falls off. I looked at Deva. He was yelling his ass off, struggling to lay his hands on Vijay. There was no mask on Deva's face; none that I could see. He was raw and real. Probably that's what attracted me to him. All these days I thought something was wrong with me as I never felt attracted to anyone. Turned out there was nothing wrong with me, I just wanted a man—a real man—definitely hard to find. But here he was!

I saw him struggling as he was being carried away by the workers. I hid behind a tall shrub as he made his way to me, angry as ever, his T-shirt crushed. He looked around for me like I was a lost child and I watched that for one whole minute and then emerged.

"There you are!" he said, heaving a sigh of relief. I came close to him and adjusted his T-shirt. He was caught off guard but he didn't stop me. His body stiffened and his eyes widened. I have to confess that I did try to feel his body and it was so fit; it felt like I was touching a rock. He moved away. I understood and backed off.

"Look, if you want to fight them, you can't do it this way," I said. He looked at me strangely as we slowly trod our way back.

"What do you mean?"

"I mean, clearly, they are powerful and twisted. They won't give a damn about a righteous man constantly yanking at them."

He nodded, his face intent. I couldn't help but smile.

"Saw how they carried you away? Like a mattai (fallen branch) of a tree on their site that is just a minor inconvenience."

"Yes. I did complain to the police and . . ."

"Oh please," I said. "You think the police, of all people, would help you? They are the easiest target when money is the bait."

"You're only saying that because you're a lawyer," he said. "Lawyers hate policemen."

"True. But look, if you gotta fight this, you gotta do it right. There is no use running about screaming, though it might seem like the only option available. But it's not. There's a way."

"What's that?"

"You have to be twisted like them. Calm like them."

"What do you mean?"

"Take your time to find dirt on them and expose it when the time is right."

"That's crazy," he said, but his pace slowed down; he was listening intently.

"Look Deva," I said. Calling an older, handsome man by his name was always a turn on. "You're a good man. But that won't get you anywhere. You'll be kicked in your butt. Or well, you'd get your butt burnt by them. In a jiffy."

He nodded, his face serious. I expected a smile.

"What do I do?"

I thought for a moment. "I could help you," I said. "Give me some time. I'll get you what you need."

He laughed. "You're sounding crazy now," he said, unable to control his laughter. "You think I'd let you get into this gutter? You have a whole life ahead of you and I don't want to put you in any danger."

"You won't," I shrugged. "Just don't let anybody know I'm working with you."

"How can you trust me? You just met me."

I smiled. "I like the chances."

The lane had ended and I had to bid farewell to him. My heart thudded as we parted and I was pretty sure he looked at me until I turned around the corner. I didn't know whether he did it because he was looking out for me or because he liked me, but either way, I liked it.

My mind was elsewhere when I sat for dinner with my mom and dad.

"Appa, I met someone called Deva today," I said, hoping he could tell me who this man was. "He said he knew you."

My dad's sullen face broke into the brightest smile I'd ever seen.

"Wow!" he started and went on and on about him. About how he had saved accident victims, fought against corrupt politicians, served as a crusader for the entire eight villages. Also, he went out to other cities to help collect funding to serve the needy.

"He is godsent," my dad concluded.

"What happened to his family?" I asked.

I came to know the terrible tragedy that had befallen him. He had a son who was in his school in a hostel away from him. His wife had passed away in a car crash on the day of her son's birthday. I felt extremely bad for him.

I couldn't sleep that night. His facial features, his voice, the creases on his forehead, his twisted mouth when he got angry, his deep eyes, his beard—everything disturbed me. Compiling this with his terribly tragic story and that being the catalyst for his urge to do the right thing just melted me, both physically and emotionally.

Though I couldn't technically name this feeling, it felt good.

7
REVELATIONS

17 January 2016
Achipatti Village

The third day of Pongal ended beautifully and soon enough, we were all back to Rudran uncle's house and so were Aadhi and uncle Deva. It was past twelve and my dad, uncle Rudran, Aadhi and uncle Deva sat in the front yard with fried groundnuts. The men were catching up on their good old days, laughing and having their bro talk, while me and Aadhi sat away from the men and spoke about our favourite books, music and stuff teenagers would talk about. The women and my cousins were fast asleep after the busy day.

Aadhi was twenty and most of the things I said made him laugh. I wasn't sure if he was laughing because of me or *at* me. But I didn't mind. His smile and laugh were too intoxicating. We had a wholesome dinner of ven Pongal with thogayal and kadhambam sambhar—the sambhar that has literally every vegetable that you can think of and tasted like a slice of heaven. At the end of every meal in Achipatti, I eat a cup of curd. Rudran or Deva uncle always made it a point to bring me a cup of fresh curd—a sign of their love. The thick, delicious curd made from fresh milk from the cows that stood in our front yard, was just something one could die for. One good thing about villages is that the food evokes certain taste buds that you had no idea existed!

The cold breeze blew gently and the early sleepers left the party to sleep. My dad was the first one to go and then Rudran uncle followed. Aadhi couldn't hold it any longer too. A big yawn from him made uncle

Deva ask him to go and sleep, and he readily agreed. He ruffled my hair lovingly as he left, or probably used my head as a support to stand up—I had no idea. But me and uncle Deva shared giggles.

"Think he likes me?" I asked, popping another groundnut.

"Have never been surer of anything in my life."

I smiled as I held my head low.

"Hey you want to have a drink?" I asked

"Now?"

"Yes. You look like you could really use one."

"Your mom would kill me if she sees her fifteen-year-old daughter serving me booze."

I laughed. "That's true. She'd kick your ass. But everyone likes having a drink now and then. I mean, who doesn't?" I said as I headed inside and grabbed a bottle of red wine from the fridge. "Just red wine. Not one of your stinky beers. We're good to go."

We were seated at the thinnai—the place that held only good memories for me. Be it the time we used to play cards or eat sugarcanes or the time me and my cousins used to talk about our latest crushes at school or the time an old lady hugged uncle Deva for helping her daughter, a place where uncle Rudran solved a lot of petty village issues or a time like this. However, the best memories were of times when uncle Deva got a little high and recounted his old stories and I listened to him with awe. It was always a treat to watch him share about his life and that was pretty much why I insisted on the glass of wine.

Uncle Deva looked a bit stooped that night. He drank glass after glass. But instead of ranting about his life that he usually did, he turned silent and figuratively, got smaller and smaller. His shoulders slumped into a heap and he rested his head on the wall, his eyes darting into oblivion.

It was hard for me to see the rigid, rugged man with his shoulders held high suddenly droop like a wilted flower. I wanted to know if he was alright. But there had been a lot of emotional conversations that day and

I had seen him cry twice since the day I met him—both times today. So I tried to lighten the mood.

"Cat got your tongue?" I asked, gently pulling the wine glass away from him. "Why not amuse me with one of those boring stories?"

He didn't budge.

"Hey," I said, patting his shoulder. They had always felt rough in my hands; like a rock. Now, though they were strong, they seemed vulnerable. Something was seriously wrong. "Uncle, what's up?"

With a start, he moved and looked for the glass of wine.

"Enough," I took it further away. "What's this about? Is this about Aadhi?"

"Nope." He said straightening up.

"Then?"

"You don't want to know."

"Then I certainly do."

He looked at me for a second and then stared blankly and smiled.

"You know she was just like you. Quite persuasive."

"Who?" I asked, confused by the sudden change in topic.

He turned silent and his face became conscious.

"Uncle," I rubbed his arm. "Who are you talking about? Your wife?"

"Yeah sure," he said and looked away. But I knew at that moment it wasn't about her. He was lying. Was uncle Deva in a relationship? Then why did he say *was* instead of *is*? I became curious, but I didn't want to push a drunken man.

"It's funny actually," he started. "For those people out there, I have done so much, right? They think I'm some kind of a saviour. You remember the old lady who came over yesterday? She told me that I'm the Lord Ayyanar she worships."

"That's awesome." I said, my mind still rephrasing what he had said. About some girl or woman.

"You're kidding, right? That's the most ridiculous thing I've ever heard. Comparing me to the glorious God who guards the entire village from all the evil forces. How silly do you think that is?"

"Well, if you ask me, it's not silly at all. That's pretty much what you do. Don't you?"

He fell silent.

"I try to do that," he said.

"There you go."

"But I'm afraid I might just fail. Those guys are… huge. Untouchable. They will bring doom. They already did, those bastards! How am I ever going to fight against them? How will I save *my* people?"

"What? Which guys? What are you talking about?"

He coughed and shook himself. "Go to sleep, kiddo. This is not something you want to know."

"Stop it. Tell me now! Who are you talking about?"

He sighed. "Veera Explosives."

"The explosives factory in our village? What about them?"

He stayed silent, his breath quickening. *Veera Explosives,* I thought. Something immediately came to mind.

"I even heard Rudran uncle talking about it yesterday," I said. "About how they have provided job opportunities for everyone in the village despite them being illiterate. Good pay with benefits. I think even the owner has visited a couple of times. Even the last Pongal, I remember. Vijay is his name, right? Vijay Kumar. Nice guy. Bought gifts and sweets for all the kids."

I hadn't noticed, but uncle Deva was growing redder with each passing statement. I even heard a low growl the moment I mentioned the word 'Vijay'.

"So that's all it takes, huh?" he asked. "Gifts and sweets? To *buy* you?"

"Woah, woah!" I said. "Easy now! I just said what I knew. And hey, he didn't buy me."

He sighed. “I'm sorry, kid. It's just the wine talking.”

“I highly doubt it. What's with you and Vijay? He didn't *buy* you gifts? Oh wait, high school rivalry? Or better. He stole your kindergarten girlfriend!”

He gave me a pained look and turned dead silent. I knew I had gone overboard.

“I'm sorry. I was just kidding,” I said and handed over the wine glass to him. “That was just a stupid defence.”

“I get it. You're smart for your age.”

“Oh, don't patronize me,” I said.

He guffawed for a second and again went back to slumping his shoulders.

“What is it, uncle?” I asked. “In all these years I haven't seen you like this. You seem weak. What is it about Vijay that's bothering you?”

“It's not Vijay alone. It's his company Veera Explosives. And what it's doing to Achipatti.”

“What do you mean?”

“If our village will ever meet its end one day, I'm pretty sure it would be because of them.”

A chill ran through my spine.

“WH ... what?”

“Their story goes way back. I still remember the day twelve years ago when a guy walked into Achipatti with such a sweet smile asking for a piece of land for his stupid fruit grove. And the village panchayats just fell for the manipulation. They fell hard. But I don't blame them. Those guys seemed harmless at that time; extremely harmless. They started the explosives factory construction two years later.” He paused for a deep inhale. “Now, they've grown so huge and untouchable and the elders who allowed them are long gone. People like me who have seen everything from the start can just drink and brood while those duffers still have the audacity to step into our homes and lure us with their stupid baits.”

"Stop it," I said. "Do not talk like this. This is not you."

I paused.

"Oh well, this is me."

"Nope," I said, pulling his chin to make him face me. "You know what I decided on the day I met you?"

"What?"

"That this is how the hero of my book should be like. He should look the way you look, walk the way you walk, talk the way you talk, consider other people's pains as his solve others' problems at ease just the way you do, and most importantly, would never give up just like you wouldn't."

He smiled at me.

"And would definitely have a killer smile like this," I said and my uncle burst into laughter.

"You're a dynamite. You know that, right?" he said.

"At times. Thanks for reminding me."

He nodded, the smile intact on his face.

"So, tell me about these guys. What's that long story? Let me hear the short version of it. What actually happened?"

My uncle nodded and began, "Something bad. Those who stood with them – the Panchayats – even their lands got severely polluted by the waste from the factory. Their well water was contaminated. So, this made them all unite and stand up against them. Not just Achipatti, but a group of eight villages that surrounded us were ready to fight against them, as the waste disposed of from their factory slowly began to affect the water. So, from each village, they elected one person to conduct the case against them. But nothing has worked till date."

"That's horrific!" I said. "I didn't think those guys were such twisted sociopaths."

"Twisted," uncle Deva shrugged and smiled. "She used to say that."

What the heck? Who on earth is 'she'?

"Did she now?" I smiled and played accordingly. My curiosity got the better of me. I didn't mind taking advantage of the drunk man.

"Yeah, she did," he rambled on. Good. "You remind me of her. Your adamancy, intelligence, stubbornness. But beyond that, the honesty, the c-care." Tears formed in his eyes and he drank a mouthful.

"Wow. She sounds interesting. What's her name? Is it the same as mine as well?"

"No. Not even close. Her name is Arch..." he stopped short. His eyes widened and he glared at me. I looked away. "You sly girl."

"Uncle," I leaned and looked at him, squeezing his stone-like arm. "Who are you talking about? You can tell me anything. You know that right?"

He heaved a deep sigh. I could smell the wine breath.

"Promise me this," he said. "You'll never ever ask me about this ever again or talk about her to anyone. If you really love me, you'll do this."

My brows raised. He looked deeply hurt and agitated. I had no idea what was causing that. I wanted to tell him he needn't have any guilt if he was in a relationship. But there was some other deep pain in him I couldn't quite put my finger to. I wished I could help him. "Okay, I won't. Trust me."

He held my hand as if grabbing a promise from me without my permission.

Sure. I could die for his secret. Whatever it might be. "Let's go back to the explosives guys," I said, changing the topic. "Don't you think they are sadists? Like they really want to hurt people?"

"Nah, nothing of the sort. They are just businessmen. They needed the money."

"This isn't the way to earn it. This is inhuman!"

"I know that, kiddo. I had that realization long back."

"When I grow up, I'll write about this. I'll write about everything in detail and thrash them."

My uncle laughed. Probably at my innocence or at my confidence; I had no idea. But I was glad he was happy.

"You will definitely become a writer, Shravya," he said and kissed my forehead. "And I'll be there to watch!"

"I know!" I said as I hugged him. "I'd introduce you to my readers. I'll tell them: 'Meet the hero of my books!'"

My uncle laughed. "I'd love that," he said.

We just smiled and stayed silent for the next few minutes, as we let the cold breeze do the talking.

"Let's get some sleep, shall we?" I said as I checked the time. "It's past two."

"Yes. And you know what? I feel light after so long."

He said and trod heavily to his room.

8
COMPLICATED LOVE. IS THERE ANY OTHER KIND?

Archana

8 October 2006 – TEN YEARS AGO
Achipatti Village

I woke up early. The events of the previous day came rushing back to me. I couldn't help but smile. I had to help him. I had to nail those sons of bitches. Pardon my language here, but my mind always throws the rawest words. It helps me think better.

It didn't take long for me to find Deva. I had asked my dad where his house was; a few farms away from ours. I collected my laptop and walked to his place. I saw him carrying a large bundle of hay, a cigarette in his mouth. He was wearing a white T-shirt, soiled as usual, this time with soil literally. I liked this better than the cement. The sun climbed higher, casting the sky with its celestial beauty and somehow made the man look like a heavenly being on earth. Sweaty, soiled, sexy and heavenly. My jaw dropped. I was wearing a dark maroon kurti, a complete contrast to my fair complexion, and my hair was pulled back and tied in a ponytail. I highlighted my eyes with kohl and my big, plump lips with a shade of lipstick matching my dress. I looked—pardon the swagger yet truth here—drop dead gorgeous.

His beard was dripping with sweat and he looked at me questioningly as he wiped his forehead. I walked into the field towards him. He could not take his eyes off me and I took the chance to push my hair strands behind my ears.

I started walking towards him, but tripped on the field's channel and was about to fall face first onto the field. I was worried about my make-up. I didn't want to fight the fall and look like a goon. I accepted the fall, turning my face sideways, but a strong pair of hands caught me.

I opened my eyes and gasped to see Deva's face so close to mine. His grip on my back was so tight that I think I heard my bones crack. I didn't mind. I wished he crushed every single one. His tanned face was so close to mine that his beard almost touched my face. His deep eyes looked right into my soul.

In an instant, he removed his hand from my back and pushed me away so hard that it almost hurt me.

"What are you doing here?" he asked, the creases back on his forehead. He was angry.

"I thought we were going to work together. Regarding nailing those muttonheads."

"Stop it. Just stop," he moved further away. I wondered why he wasn't finding my joke funny today. He did yesterday.

"What?"

"I can't bring you into this. Just leave."

"But I want to help you."

"I don't need your help."

"You won't win in this way. They'll crush you."

"Then so be it," he glared at me. "Let me be crushed. I don't want anyone else crushed for my sake."

"Your sake? I'm a frigging lawyer."

"You're just a student."

"Topper of my university. Already got the license to practice. I have decided to pick up this case."

"Stop this," he said. "Just stop."

He turned his back and went towards his house. It was big, certainly bigger than ours.

"Can I come in for a glass of water at least?" I called after him. He turned back, glared for one whole minute and nodded. I smiled and sprinted towards the house.

* * *

The walls were plain. There were pictures of his son all around the house, but none of his wife. Usually, people don't put out pictures of the dead. I wondered why. Maybe it was too painful for him. Was he over her? The thought sent a shudder down my back. He came back with a *sombu* full of water. We Tamilians do not believe in glass tumblers. We believe in sombu—a pot-like vessel, which can be hand held. It felt like one was drinking water only if it was from a sombu. No sipping, just open the mouth wide, look up and gulp down the contents.

Pure bliss.

I wanted to do that but I didn't want to look like a frigging cow. I sipped like a cute school girl. He looked away and sighed. I knew I was pushing too hard by being forthcoming. I placed the sombu down on the teapoy.

"Why are you doing this?" he asked.

"Doing what?"

"Trying to help me?"

"Like I said, I'm a lawyer."

"Don't give me that crap," he said. "You think I don't know?"

"Know what?"

He paused and looked at me, giving me a pained expression.

"You ... uh ... I think you want to pursue me." He gazed down.

I burst into laughter. I couldn't hold it. He looked so cute when he said that—like a guilty school kid.

"Maybe," I agreed. Usually, I'm a timid person. But somehow, all my inner confidence, buried deep down my soul erupted and splashed out when I saw this man. Love does that to you, I guess.

"That's the reason you want to go after the Veera Explosives guys. To get close with me."

"Yes."

He seemed taken aback by the directness.

"I don't know what to say."

"Do you like me?" I asked.

He was caught off guard. His eyes widened still.

"I have a son."

"I didn't hear a no."

"You're just twenty-three. A kid!"

"Still didn't hear a no."

"You're crazy. And so young!"

"You're thirty-five. I'm not that younger than you. And stop calling me a kid. I want to puke every time you say that."

His facial muscles relaxed a bit. A tiny smile emerged. My knees buckled.

"Also, the reason I want to help you is not just because I like you. It's because I can *really* help you."

"How's that?"

"Look."

I brought out my laptop and showed him the presentation I had made on Veera Explosives.

"Veera Explosives was a start-up corporation. Four people co-owned it. Ramachandran, a small-time farmer who rose during the upsurge of onion prices, Vijay Kumar's father Jagan Kumar, Achyuth Mohan, an industrialist, and a big-time goon from Coimbatore North, Gunashekaran." I started showing their pictures on the screen. I swiped to the next slide. "In mid-1995, Ramachandran, originally based in Salem, walked into our village claiming he needed a few acres of land to start his fruit grove and plantations, and he offered a good sum for it. Considering his reputation for maintaining good farms, the poor, unsuspecting farmers gave away their lands."

"I remember this," Deva said. "I was a teenager back then, but I remember the panchayat meetings being held."

I nodded. "But not one step was taken to start that fruit grove. And three years later, in 1998, without anyone knowing, he and his accomplices got the NOC from the government to start their explosives factory. However, when they wanted more space for godowns to store the required chemicals, they had to get permission from the village panchayats. A lot of people were against this."

"Including my dad," Deva said. "They argued that this would pollute the water table tremendously. They also said that the only reason an explosives factory wanted to step into Achipatti was because of our pure, unpolluted water which is available at ease. Producing explosives needs a lot of clean water."

"There you go," I smiled at him, pointing to my slide on the water table contamination. "But they, with their sugar-coated words, presented an argument that they were just going to produce the chemicals required only for fireworks and that it was harmless as day. They even had their members bring out models to show how the chemicals were produced and how they were harmless. They also mentioned that the guys who were against it were purely overreacting. The panchayats got carried away with the show of all the so-called technology and sided with them."

"Wow. You speak as if you were there. I remember all of this. Hell, I was a part of the discussion. Well, I just watched them discuss."

"And in 2005, they started their construction," I ignored him. "They started taking advantage of our people's leniency and broke all the government-laid rules. According to the bye-laws, there shouldn't be any public buildings or houses in the vicinity of at least 1300 metres of the factory. But the Kamarajar colony is only 300 metres away, and the government school built in 1904 is at a distance of 600 metres from it!

Hell, every hospital, bank, post office and even the EB office lies within 1300 metres of the building. But the worst thing is, they occupied the five-acre seventy-two cent land that belonged to *mandhai veli.* As you know it is the land ..."

"Allocated only for grazing purposes. For the cows." He finished. I nodded.

"Yes. And they occupied the path leading up to the Manmalai Perumal temple on top of Senthoor hill—one of the prominent hills in Western Ghats."

He gazed intently at the screen.

"All the four guys who started the company were bad news. Too rich. Well connected. One of them is a rowdy for crying out loud," I pointed to the smiling face of a man on the screen. Everything about him was fat. His bulky sagging face, his eyes drawn in due to the fat around, his enormous man boobs that he didn't care to hide, and his even enormous belly. The smile on his face was huge. But his eyes did not smile. They were in a completely opposite zone. Evil, I'd say, if I could be more dramatic. He wore a shiny purple kurta. So shiny that one could almost see their face reflecting on it.

"Those eyes," Deva said, squinting at them. "Bad news, indeed. Backs your theory."

"Has North Coimbatore under his fat thumb." I said, raising a brow at him to depict the fat man's grandeur.

"Can't disagree."

"You remember the time when there was a roaring hike in onion prices?" I asked.

"Sure do. Can't forget the time when our sambhars were more tomatoey and less tasty."

"Five months ago, our guy here decided to grow onions in his twenty acres of land. A lucky swine."

He frowned at my choice of words. I shrugged.

"Became a millionaire in the shortest period of time. He was all over the news."

"No wonder Vijay's family are in a partnership with him—to woo people of the villages using his name." Deva said as he tried to use the mouse. It was cute. He was an old man who didn't know how to use computers and yet, was curious like a child. I just wanted to hug that man and never let him go. I swallowed my overwhelming emotions with a cough.

"The industrialist and Vijay's father come from money. Nothing special about them," I said.

"Nice."

"This is just basic research that I did overnight. But I want to get to the depth. Catch them in the act with proper stats and everything. In a way that they won't have space to argue at all. In a way we could ruin them forever."

He sat there devoid of words. His mouth hung open as he eyed my computer screen. I waited with a proud little smile on my face as I adored his features. The jawline, the beard that was now dry, those unfindable lips, the dark complexion, the eyes. Those deep eyes that looked deeper now with concentration. My heart thudded.

"I can't believe this. I had no idea about this," he said and I was brought back to sense.

"There is something else," I said. "See this man?" I pointed to the screen.

He squinted.

The picture was taken at a random event; seemed like some gallery opening. Vijay stood there surrounded by a few people. I pointed to a tall, dark, well-built man among the people. He was nowhere close to Vijay. He was far away, probably trying to hide himself among people, but he stood out as he was taller and more muscular than anyone else and had the bodyguard vibe about him. The kind that looked like he could beat the shit out of anyone, anytime. He had his eyes on Vijay the way a hawk stared at its prey. There was a noticeable snake tattoo on his arm.

"See this?" I showed him another picture. This time it was another gathering. "Here." Again, the muscular man was right there, his eyes fixated on Vijay. It looked like he hated blinking. Again, he stood far away from him.

"And here."

Another picture at a public event where he was right there, a few feet away.

"What's his name?"

"I don't know. I couldn't find out."

"Do you think he's the bodyguard?" Deva asked.

"Maybe." I looked away, thoughtful.

"What?" He narrowed his eyes at me.

"If Vijay is more of what you projected, and if what my instinct said about him the other day is right ... well, if he is actually an evil, heartless villain who doesn't care about people, then this man," I pointed to the snake tattoo, "is more than *just* a bodyguard."

The air turned chilly.

"Then what is he?" Deva spoke in a whisper. I bet he felt the chills too. It was like a physical being in the room.

"I think he is more of," I paused, "an executor."

The hairs on my neck stood the moment I said the word. I imagined all sorts of horrible things he would have been made to do. Did he do it with pleasure? He did look the sort. But what if he was a poor innocent orphan who found the wrong path? I guess we'd never know. I let the thought slide.

"An executor?"

"Yeah."

"You mean, a hit-man?" he asked.

"Call it whatever," I said. "But this man is the one who does the job for him. For Vijay."

"And you know this how?"

"I'm a lawyer. I can sniff stuff. I'm very sure that if Vijay needs someone dead," I said, "this tattooed man does it for him."

Silence. He kept glaring at the picture.

"And we know nothing about him?" he asked.

"It's like he never existed," I said. "No virtual trail. Nothing. I think he doesn't even have an identity. Mostly Vijay keeps him anonymous, takes care of him and uses him for the dirty work."

He nodded. I shut the laptop own. The room seemed normal again.

"See?" I smiled and heaved a deep sigh. "Told you. I can help you."

He looked at me. I don't know if it was imagination or it happened for real but I swear he was checking out my features as I smiled. My eyes first, and then my lips. My breath got caught in my throat. He looked into my eyes again and I held my breath.

"Okay," he said, looking away and shaking himself a little. "But promise me one thing."

"Shoot."

"You should stay anonymous. You should never ever reveal your involvement in this to anyone. Not even your parents. Our meetings should be discreet."

"Done. Happily."

He gave a glare. I smiled at him like the North Coimbatore goon. An evil smile. He controlled his chuckle, or so I thought.

"And one more thing," he said, his face turning dull in the fraction of a second. I wonder how he did that.

"Shoot."

"Don't fall for me," he said. "You'll regret it."

"Too late for that."

"You don't understand."

"You still love your wife."

"Of course I do!"

I swallowed whatever was finding its way up my throat and asked the one question I couldn't say out loud without feeling the heaviness of a boulder on my shoulder. "You're not over her?"

He stayed silent.

"Oh," I said, as the wave of realization hit me, "you are. You have accepted her death, but," I paused as a few more waves hit me, "you're not over the guilt."

More silence.

"Got it. You blame yourself for her death," I said, grabbing all that from his expression. I'm good at reading faces. Darn good indeed. And his face, I could read forever.

"Stop it," he said.

"Whatever," I replied. "I really like you and I won't stop pursuing you. I have never felt this way about anyone in my life. I'm quite competitive and I usually achieve what I want. And till now, I've never wanted something as badly as I want you. You think I'll let you go?" I asked.

He just stood there, his eyes fixed on me. Then he forced himself to look away and then he looked back at me. I think a part of him was adoring me, a part of him wanted me but the rest was guilt tripping him, telling him to not even look at me.

I smiled at him.

9
THE HUG

18 January 2016
Achipatti Village

The sun broke into my room through the windows and I twisted and turned. What uncle had said about Veera Explosives was bugging me pretty bad. I wanted to meet him and speak to him about it. I wanted to do something; anything to help him fight against those guys. It probably was pretty naïve of me, but it was worth a try.

"Aww," my sister, Shriya said, jumping on the bed. "Looks like you woke up pretty early today."

"Yeah, so?"

"Let's plan out what we are going to do?"

"What do you mean? For Pongal? I thought the last day was pretty much a no show."

"Really?" she asked. "You really don't know?"

"Know what?"

"It's Aadhi's birthday tomorrow. We've got to plan something for twelve o'clock tonight."

"How do you know?"

"I was ransacking cupboards looking for my top and found his licence instead."

A chill ran through my veins.

No. no.

Tomorrow is the day my uncle's wife passed. And as usual, he was going to ice his son out.

"You're right," I said. "We should plan something nice."

"Yay! I'd be the organizer! You just sit and watch, milady," Shriya squealed and left the room.

* * *

I heard from dad that uncle Deva had woken up early and left for his house. Good. Now I can plan out everything without him finding out anything. I had to find a proper location for the birthday. My mind was busy and my appetite was long gone. But one long stare from my mom made me rethink my decision.

I had my breakfast of idlis and three different kinds of chutneys—mint, tomato and groundnuts—coupled with spicy sambhar. The food was insanely tasty, and it immediately lifted my spirits. I decided on what to do next. An idea struck me. Who knows Achipatti well enough to suggest a good place for me?

I went to my uncle Rudran's farm and found him working hard along with the workers. I waved to him and pointed to the farm house, which marked the centre of the clearing

Within a few minutes, my uncle was there with a big smile on his sweaty face.

"What brings you here so early in the day, Shravya?" he asked. "Want some curd?" he laughed at his own joke.

"Good one," I said. "And there's plenty left at your home. That ain't why I'm here."

"So why are you here?" he asked.

"Tomorrow is Aadhi's birthday and I want your idea on what to do at midnight and where."

Uncle Rudran's face fell.

"That's a bummer. Deva wouldn't want to come."

"That's exactly why I want to do this. I want to fix it."

"Believe me. I have tried everything."

"Let me try once," I said.

"Persuasion. Good. Works every time."

"Thanks," I said. "I need you to tell me a perfect spot for the party. Something private, something scenic, something divine and beautiful, something peaceful. Something like a 'go to' place when you're down."

My uncle smiled as his eyes shone.

"You know what?" he said. "I have just the place."

* * *

I panted hard as I took the steps up the hill.

"Wait up, I think I'm going to pass out," I said as Rudran uncle sprinted in front of me like a horse.

"You're fine. Just don't stop."

"I'm trying!" I screamed as he was getting out of sight.

It took me half an hour more to reach what looked like the final rock that marked the edge of this hill.

"Come on," uncle said. "See for yourself!"

I took my last step and the moment I let my gaze fall on the summit, my eyes grew wide and my heart beat fast. Joy brimmed in me. The whole place looked right out of a storybook. There was a huge, dreamy banyan tree in front of me that seemed to protect the entire peak and the shrubs that grew in its care. Its trunk was home to algae of the most beautiful shade of green. The ground was moist and looked like a green mat was laid out on it – like a lawn that was mowed regularly. The edge of the hill overlooked the entire village. I could even see Rudran uncle's farm and the farmhouse that stood at the centre. And most importantly, I could see green everywhere, from the mountain—the canopy of trees that beautified Achipatti—were all visible from here.

The wind blew gently. It was surprisingly moist.

"My God!" I said. "What is this place?"

"A slice of heaven," my uncle said.

On my right, there was a flight of stairs. "What is this, uncle?"

"This leads to the Rangarajar temple on top."

"There's a temple? Here?" I squealed in disbelief.

"Yes. Come up," he said.

I did so and soon enough, I saw a structure barely standing—it had no doors, only two walls and a barely fitting roof. On my left was a big boulder with a niche on it. Near it was a tall *karungali vel*—the iron rod that signified the one that belonged to Lord Muruga. It looked so majestic. I stepped inside to see a broken idol of Lord Rangaraja's sleeping pose and below it were a lot of diyas.

"The people from our village come here to pray," said uncle Deva. "It's their belief that everything that they wish for from here always comes true."

"That's beautiful," I said.

"Come out here," he said and headed out from the back entrance where a single boulder sat at the edge, marking the end of the hill, overlooking the entire village. The view was amazing and I sat on the boulder, almost tumbling back from the wind.

"Like it?" My uncle sat beside me, with his heavy arm around my shoulder.

"Love it," I smiled.

* * *

It was all arranged by the end of the day. Very simple, yet so beautiful. Shriya and I took the bus to Pollachi and bought two dozen paper lanterns along with glowing LED pillars to light up the space. Uncle Deva and Aadhi had to meet some villagers for urgent work and that was good. That had kept them out of the house. We first decided to keep the party private—just uncle Rudran's family, my family, uncle Deva and his son. But then, Deva uncle's friends and a few boarding school friends of Aadhi and my grandmother and the other aunts decided they wanted to surprise

Aadhi, too. That wasn't the issue. I was just worried as none of the aunts were good at keeping secrets. They were known for their juicy gossip and I knew one of them would directly break the plan to Aadhi. Hence, after Aadhi came back home, I wanted to keep him out till the evening.

As it was the end of Pongal, Aadhi wore an olive-green shirt and *veshti*—the traditional Tamil attire, and he looked so darn hot. His height complimented the attire even more, and he looked so fresh and handsome, especially with the *vibhuthi* on his forehead. I did not know if my girly instincts were stirred, but I felt a strange physical sensation every time he came near me, or when his hand brushed against mine or when I lay my eyes on his thick beard and his thin lips hidden by it or when I inhaled his intoxicating manly scent unpolluted by any perfume. And that was becoming my most favourite scent in the world!

I took him to the fields, to the well and we walked and walked on the lanes of Achipatti, having chips, ice cream, kulfi, and talking about everything. It was so easy to make Aadhi do things my way. I wanted him to be distracted and he was, willingly, happily. He just wanted to spend time with me and the more I did that, the harder I was falling for him.

Dusk engulfed the village like a mild blanket of navy-blue and black. My heart raced as within hours I would know if my epic plan would be that way or turn into an epic failure. It was 9 p.m. and I still didn't want to risk taking Aadhi to Rudran uncle's home.

"We'll eat outside," I said to him. He had been smiling since we stepped out.

"Yes," he readily agreed, with a bigger smile. "Definitely."

"I know a place here that makes the best ever parottas. You'd be addicted for life," I said, pulling his arm in the other direction.

"Sure, anything you say."

We reached the parotta place. It was just a barrow with a happy man behind it and happy customers in front of it, gulping down their delicacies.

"Anna, two sets parotta with chicken kurma," I ordered, pushing my way through the men. But Aadhi was right behind me, fortifying me like a soldier, making sure nobody's body touched mine. Right out of Danielle Steel's books!

Oh damn!

I got two plates of steaming kurma and parotta and we sat at one of the plastic tables. Aadhi didn't seem to mind the mess. In fact, it looked like he was relishing every moment with me—taking it in slowly, and enjoying it bit by bit. I had no idea what I had ever done to make a guy be this attracted to me. All I knew was that I was a dumb, okay-looking girl. But he made me feel like I was some princess from a faraway land. I tore the crispy parotta, dipped it in the kurma, tore a piece of chicken and put it on his plate. He immediately grabbed it and ate it. His eyes sparkled.

"This is awesome!" he said, reaching for a bigger bite. I couldn't help but gaze at the hypnotizing motion of his bearded jaw.

A few minutes passed and I noticed him smile at me time and again.

"What?" I asked when I caught him for the umpteenth time looking at me and smiling without reason.

"What, Shravya?" he smiled again.

"Why are you smiling?"

"You're so adorable," he said. "Especially with the parotta adorning your chin."

"Oh jeez," I said and wiped my face. He laughed some more but in a second, his face grew serious.

"I like you, Shravya," he said point blank. Just like that. Without any warning. Right to my parotta-smeared face. "I really do."

"I do, too," I said, not knowing what else to say. "I thought it was obvious. We had spent the last five hours together. That doesn't happen if we don't like someone, right? Unlike your dad who spends countless hours with his enemies."

"You're changing the topic," he said. "You know exactly what I mean."

"What do you expect me to say, Aadhi? I'm just fifteen for god's sake."

"Yeah, I'll wait until you and I are old enough."

I guffawed. "Don't be silly," I said, even though my heart went out to him and I was on the brink of tears. These would be the words every girl would die to hear, and here I was, receiving exactly that, but unable to handle it.

"I'm not silly. I promise you today that I'll wait for you."

"I don't like this conversation. Not even one bit."

"I know that," he said. "But I couldn't hold it back. Sorry it came tumbling out...I couldn't help it."

"It's alright," I checked the time. It was ten thirty. It would be the right time to start walking towards the hill. The plan was to lure Aadhi onto the hill without making him suspect a thing. That was my job. And Shriya's job was to somehow fool uncle Deva into believing that some teenage punk had messed with her saying she can't reach the hill at midnight. We decided to go with this story as we knew too well that uncle Deva, who would go to any lengths for me or for her, would take this as a personal hit and make her win this challenge.

"Let's show that punk a piece of us," were his words after he wiped Shriya's crocodile tears. She gave a thumbs up to me when I was about to step out with Aadhi. She was an emotionless ghoul, and a class actor.

"Hey Aadhi," I said. "I would like to take you somewhere," I said and paused, considering the awkward conversation between us just a few moments ago. "If you'd like to accompany me."

I played it safe and prayed he would say yes.

"Of course!" he said and the same old smile was back again, but this time, tainted a little with pain. That broke my heart.

"It's a small hill opposite uncle Rudran's farm. It looks beautiful at this time of night. Can we go?"

"Shravya," he said and stopped in his path and looked right into my eyes—in a deep, intense way and I thought he was going to kiss me. "I would go anywhere with you. You don't have to say where."

"That's uh…" I paused, stepping back, "very sweet."

It took us one hour to reach the hill. The time was 11:40 p.m. Twenty minutes more and my heart raced. But Aadhi was caught in the moment, looking in awe at the tree, the moon and the flight of stairs near us.

"Wow!" he said. "How did you even know about this place?"

Before I could answer, I could hear footsteps—heavy, big ones and tiny quick ones nearby. It was Deva uncle and Shriya. Gosh, we had to hide. Aadhi hadn't the slightest clue about the footsteps as he was marvelling at the view from the edge of the hill behind the tree.

"Aadhi, come," I said and pulled him up the stairs. "Come with me, quick!"

He obliged happily and soon enough, we were at the wall-less temple. I pulled him out to the boulder and sat with him, hoping the others were right on time to set up the place for our arrival.

"Wow! Would you look at this?" he said, his palms on his bearded face.

"Yeah, yeah, very pretty. Look up! The stars are cool, too," I said, panicking as I heard more footsteps. An unsuspecting Aadhi lay on his back and gazed at the stars.

"Wow!" he said again. "You're right."

I wondered what I had done to deserve this guy. My panic vanished and I lay down beside him, my heart beating fast. He extended his arm so that I could rest my head on it. I contemplated whether to take it or not, even though I knew too damn well that I was going to. I lay on his strong arm, moved closer to him and gazed up at the stars. It was magical. The breeze, his arm, his beard brushing my face and the stars – everything was magical. He turned his head towards my side and so did I. He gazed right into my eyes, that killer smile long gone. Our faces were inches apart, and I swear I moved half an inch closer and he froze. This moment was absolutely magical.

Until I heard those tiny footsteps heading up the stairs.

Shriya, I thought. I sprang up with a start, darted across the temple and reached the stairs right in time to meet her.

"Hey, is he with you?" she asked.

"Shush!" I said. "He's behind the temple."

She threw a sarcastic smile. "What were you guys doing?" she whispered.

"Nothing. We could have if you hadn't walked in, you fool!" I whispered back.

"There's still time," she said. "Go back, do your stuff and come."

"Shut up, you brat," I said. "I'll bring him. You go down."

"As you wish. Use this extra time wisely. Kiss him," she said and headed down. I couldn't help but smile as I reached the boulder and saw him sitting with slumped shoulders just like his dad.

"Hey," I said.

"Did I make you uncomfortable?" he said, his face forlorn. "If so, I'm so sorry."

"No!" I said, "not at all."

"You know you just ran away." He threw up his hands like a kid.

"I uh…wanted to pee," I said and immediately regretted my reply. "The parotta, you know…squeezes the bladder."

Damn. Made it worse.

But he nodded understandingly.

"You're okay now?" he asked with an innocent face. I could just kiss him right then and there.

"Yes. Let's go back," I said, tugging his arm. "To the banyan tree. We'll sit there for a while before going down."

"Sure," he said and got up, even though I knew that he wanted to stay there. Every time he did this—every time he listened to me without any questions, I was insanely drawn to him.

We went down the stairs and soon reached the clearing. My jaw dropped open. The entire place was filled with the warm LED lamps that we had bought. The string lights were tied around the banyan tree and the table in the middle on which stood a huge chocolate cake—baked by my mother and grandmother. All around the table stood our entire family and Aadhi's friends all singing the birthday song in Tamil and clapping with josh.

Aadhi's face was blank. Only his eyes widened with each second.

One man stood away from the table, near the banyan tree, with a crestfallen face—uncle Deva. He looked confused and excited, but at the same time, he looked stuck. My heart warmed towards him. The fact that he was supposed to be happy on the day that wrecked him and tore his life apart wasn't something anyone could accept easily.

Aadhi's eyes darted in search of his father. And finally, when he found him, his lips puckered and his breaths quickened. It was obvious that he was worried about his father; worried that the bad memories might rush back because of his birthday. Aadhi smiled at everyone, said a big thank you and sprinted towards his dad and stood in front of him. The cheerful crowd held their breaths. The air suddenly turned cold. Nobody knew what to do, and I was stuck on the stairs, far away from the two men.

Deva uncle's eyes were fixed on his son's face and they immediately turned glassy. I couldn't see Aadhi's face but suddenly, he wept and jumped into his father's arms. Uncle Deva held him tight, crying on his shoulder. Both the men hugged and cried their hearts out and it was a beautiful sight. Nobody in the crowd could hold their tears back.

The way uncle Deva and Aadhi held on to each other—so tight and for so long—only proved that they had never done it in their entire lives. And the fact that they cried for so long only showed that the duo had never once together mourned the passing of the most important person in their life. This moment was certainly a release for both of them.

Aadhi being able to comfort his dad and uncle Deva slowly shedding his guilt—all through one hug!

My heart brimmed with joy, but just like the others, I stayed put. Finally, after the two let go of each other, everyone clapped hard and so did I. Everyone swarmed towards the duo and hugged them.

"Happy birthday, my son," uncle Deva said, kissing Aadhi's forehead. "And…" he paused and swallowed hard, twice. "I'm so sorry, da." He joined his palms and bowed to his son.

"No, Appa!" Aadhi held his father's palms. "You've been the best dad a guy could ask for. I love you. You're my hero!"

Deva uncle broke down in his son's arms.

And they hugged again, though their eyes were teary, this time, their faces were filled with the brightest smiles I had ever seen.

* * *

Aadhi stood in front of the cake table and we all cheered as he cut his first cake in twenty years. Uncle Deva filmed the moment, but he had to hand the mobile over to me as Aadhi fed him the first piece of the cake. He fed me the second, which was totally unexpected for me and I could tell from their faces that it was shocking for everyone else as well. His friends giggled and Shriya clapped.

Half an hour went by and we all sat together and had our cakes and snacks on the summit of the hill, playing antakshari. Aadhi sat near me, heaved a sigh and whispered a thank you into my ears.

"I really didn't expect this," he said. "This is certainly the best day of my life."

"It's my pleasure," I said and winked at him. He held my hand, and together, with our family, we lay back on the beautifully lit summit of our hill and we talked and talked until we all fell asleep on the moist green grass, without even realizing that the dawn had seeped its way through the sky and hurled itself on the top of the hill.

10
LOVE AND WORK

Archana

TEN YEARS AGO...

We started hanging out after that. Discreetly, as he might put it. Magical, as I would put it. I had impressed him with my quick research, sure. I pretended it was quick, but only I knew it took hours on my end. Two hours on the internet, one hour on call with my mentor from college, one hour to find out the lawyer who worked with people who was associated with people, who in turn worked with or were related to Vijay. And three hours to sort the research and craft the *quick* presentation I had impressed Deva with.

I had done most of the work that night. I did not know what else to do afterward. So, I decided to lull him with technical terms for a few days to make him believe I was on to something, while the truth was that I was onto him. Pretty low of me. But the things we do for love! Always fair.

I even got him a burner phone to make things more dramatic. You should have seen his face when he received it. Like an attentive first bencher learning algebra. Frankly, I did not care about my safety. First off, these Veera guys weren't as bad as Deva had projected it. They were just an explosives factory that was growing rapidly, expanding its role especially in Coimbatore city because of the market. They had chosen Achipatti because of its isolated nature and fertility. Nothing fishy there. Every factory looks for that. But yeah, they did not care about the environment like any other factories. The villagers should have stopped them before they came in but now it was too late. However, it wouldn't hurt to try and stop them now, and I was ready to try every goddamn thing to make this man happy.

But Veera Explosives had political connections. Going against them in one swing was extremely dangerous; to a point where one could lose their life. But I was still ready to do that—for a man I met yesterday!

How? No idea! I had always looked down upon people in love. They do the stupidest things and have the audacity to justify those in the name of love. And here I was, doing worse. Guess God does that to you to shut you up.

I had pinged him on his burner to visit me on top of a small hill that was a few hundred metres away from his farm. I had the habit of finding places that were 'discreet' and invited him to meet me there. He did so, with no questions asked, and with the curiosity of a cat.

It was late afternoon and he arrived with food. He always did. This time it was lemon rice and potato fry that he had cooked as I had an aversion to outside food.

"This is so good," I said as I chewed hard. The potato curry was so spicy—the way I loved it. And the lemon rice was the kind we get in temples—the highest cadre of lemon rice for a Tamilian.

He gave a nod.

"What are we up to today?" he asked.

"Not much. Let's just revise what he already collected. Find something we missed." I chewed harder. The food was so good that my stomach rumbled harder with each mouthful though I wasn't hungry at all.

He narrowed his eyes.

"You called me here for nothing?"

"I wouldn't say that," I said.

"Come on."

"Okay. I just wanted to see you. Is that so wrong?" I put the tiffin box down though I craved for more. The adrenaline rushes had begun and I couldn't eat.

"Here we go again," he sighed. "I asked you to stop that."

"Told you it's too late."

"It's been just a week since you met me. How can you speak like that?"

"I don't know. I seriously don't. I just know that the moment I saw you I felt what I had never felt before. Your righteousness, ruggedness, anger, the truth in you, the rawness in you, the rigid outer covering harbouring so much sweetness inside you, so much pain inside you, that I wish I made it disappear somehow. Your face, your body, your deep eyes that crush me with every look of yours. I could go on, you know? Everything is disturbing me so much. Physically and emotionally, and I have never felt like this before. All I know is that I would go to any extent for you. You're raw and real and I want this."

He swallowed hard. I reached into my laptop bag and produced a passport size pic and handed it to him. He received it slowly, his mind still processing my monologue.

"It's a picture of you?"

"Yes. Turn it around," I said. He did so.

I had scribbled something on the back.

Archana Deva.

I bet his throat closed, because he was trying again and again to swallow, but it wouldn't go down. He looked at me hard, his crushing look melting away. He battled for words. A teardrop escaped my eye and I realized it later. He moved closer and my heart thudded.

"I'm older than you," he said.

"You've said that so many times. Is there any other reason that you have?"

He stayed silent.

"Thought so. Just tell me this. Do you not like me? Age, children and failed marriages apart."

"I did not have a failed marriage," his voice turned stiff.

"Sorry, didn't mean that," I paused. "You know what I meant."

He nodded.

"Do you not like me?" I asked again, more like a kitten this time. He said nothing. He just sat there, breathing hard, looking at me with a yearning, yet with pain. I moved closer to him. I thought he would push me away or move away. None of that happened. He just sat there, his eyes looking deep into mine. His eyes still held pain; a lot of it, and it transferred a dull ache to me. I felt bad. I wished I knew what he was thinking about—his dead wife? His son? His quest for righteousness? The fact that he was attracted to me but I was young? What conquered his thoughts at that moment? I had no idea. But I moved closer, my lips inches away from him. A strand of his rough beard tickled my chin. My limbs quaked.

"No," he moved away gently. Just a tad, not too much. And the 'no' was so quiet. Like whispering.

"It's alright. One kiss wouldn't hurt," I spoke as quietly as him.

"No," he repeated. "I should go." He got up. My chest burned with mixed feelings.

"Stay," I said meekly. "Please."

He turned around to look at me, gave me a pained look, heaved a deep, long sigh and stood with his head hung low.

"Can you kiss me?" I asked and my directness made his eyes widen and his jaw went slack. "Let this be the first and final. I would never ask for anything else from you. I need it. I don't know if asking this as a girl to a man seems needy or slutty even."

"No," he interrupted, "do not talk like that."

"Come on, I don't even know what you're thinking. But listen, I just want to kiss you. I'm so forthcoming about this because it's what my mind needs more than my body needs it."

He continued looking at me.

"Can you?" I asked. "It would be our little secret."

He stood there, looked at me continuously, his face devoid of any expression. Then he turned his back and walked downhill.

11
THE INCIDENT

19 January 2016

The days of Pongal were over and we had to leave. This was the hardest part—saying goodbyes. Especially to uncle Deva. Every time the car pulled away from Rudran uncle's house, uncle Deva stood there watching it until it curved on the end of the lane. Just watching it, no waving, nothing.

And this time, it was worse. There were two people standing together, watching the car. Uncle Deva and Aadhi. I couldn't help but burst into tears silently, making sure that my parents didn't notice me. Shriya did, and rubbed my back.

"Shhh," she said. "It's okay. We can come here whenever we want."

I nodded. We barely talked on the way back. Guess this Pongal had a hard-hitting effect on everyone. The lanes that looked extremely pretty on the way to Achipatti barely looked pleasing on the way back. Probably it's all in our heads—the beauty of nature, the miracles of lives—it all changed with our perspective, our mindset.

The next few days after I reached home were pretty dull. Every time I went back home after spending time in Achipatti, I entered a mode of numbness and monotony. I went to school, came back, did school work, ate, slept and the cycle repeated. Time with my family was also nice, but however, when I lay on my bed at night, I replayed what had happened in Achipatti. And this time, there was someone new on the scene in my head—Aadhi.

* * *

1 December 2016

Months had passed. I was busy with my half-yearly tests and I had just returned home from school. My mom had made crispy pakodas for the evening and I polished them away with hot coffee, sitting in the balcony, watching the traffic. The mild, irritating hum of the vehicles was always so comforting and I just loved drowning myself and my thoughts deep into it.

I took a sip of the coffee and bit the pakoda, the spiciness dangling with the hotness of the coffee. It was refreshing.

"Social Science tomorrow?" my mom asked, patting my back.

"Yes."

"Good. You'll do well."

I sat to study in an hour and soon enough, I got engulfed in colonisation, the East India Company, the Dandi march and so on. I didn't realize that I had been studying for hours. When I checked the time, it was midnight.

"Woah!" I said to myself. That was when I heard my dad's mobile ring.

Who is calling at this hour? I thought and I went to the dining table to pick up the mobile. It was Rudran uncle. Figuring it must be something important, I ran into the bedroom and woke my dad, who, as usual, woke up as if thunder had fallen into the bedroom. I think it's a dad thing—to wake up as if their asses were on fire. But it's always a daughter's thing to calm their dads down with love. And as usual, after comforting him by rubbing his chest and shoulder and assuring that nothing had happened, I passed on the mobile to him and said that Rudran uncle was calling.

He picked up the phone, stood up and went to the hall to talk.

His face grew tighter and tighter with each word he heard from the other end. His lips puckered and the lines on his forehead spawned more lines. But he never said a word. I grew panicky. He ended the call and I held his hand.

"What, daddy?" I asked him. "What happened? What did he say?"

He heaved a sigh, pulled a chair from the dining table and collapsed on it.

"Daddy!" I shrieked. "What is it? Please tell me!"

"There was a blast," he said, "in Achipatti."

"Blast? What blast? I don't get you."

"At Veera Explosives factory. One building just exploded."

A chill ran through my spine as uncle Deva's story about Veera Explosives rushed through my mind. My heart thumped in my chest and my palms were sweating.

"And?" I asked. "Is everyone okay?"

"No," my dad said, "They found the remains of a lot of bodies. And the worst thing is, we don't even know how many are dead."

That instant I felt my brain slip into numbness.

12
VEERA EXPLOSIVES

2 December 2016

My dad decided to leave for Achipatti early the next morning. I had to sit for my exam the next day. He ordered me and my mom to stay in Coimbatore but he knew his words would fall on deaf ears if I had made up my mind on something. My mom obliged though. I knew there wouldn't be anything that I'd be able to do but I just had to be with Deva uncle. I knew he'd be more devastated than angry. Also, I worried that he would go into that state of numbness and shock—just the way he sat staring into oblivion right before he started talking about Veera Explosives on the day of Pongal.

My dad took the final turn to Rudran uncle's house and the moment we entered the street, a lot of people came and surrounded us, weeping and beating their chests and one of the old men fell at my father's feet.

"Help us, anna!" he cried. "My son has been blasted to pieces. You know what they did, anna? Those heartless policemen? They asked me to identify his body parts."

The man wept, holding my dad's leg tight. My dad's breaths turned jerky and he instantly pulled the man up and hugged him.

"I'm so sorry. That's horrible," he said as tears emerged effortlessly from his eyes. "We are there, ayya. We are there."

Rudran uncle came out and escorted my dad inside, gently pulling the old man away.

"What is all this, Rudran?" my dad asked, anger surging in his voice. "What the heck happened? And where on earth is Deva? Is he alright?"

"We have no idea what happened, anna!" Rudran said. "We got a call from the lawyer's family who lives a few kilometres away from the factory. They said that there was a deafening sound of a blast as if something was being bombed, and in an instant their empty cow shed was crushed by a concrete block which flew out of nowhere. They stepped out to see what was happening but a cloud of cement dust had fogged the view. They immediately called Deva and me. I have no idea where Deva is. I've tried his cell so many times."

"This is all very frustrating," my dad said, burying his head in his palms.

A villager in a lungi and a vest came running towards Rudran uncle and my dad.

"Deva anna is there at the factory," he said, panting. "He got into a fight with Vijay. You should go there now, anna!"

* * *

"You stay here!" my dad said to me. "This is an order!"

"No daddy, I'm coming along."

"No way. I don't want those scumbags to see you and you shouldn't see something like that. Things get ugly."

"I know."

"This isn't one of your stories."

"I know that too."

Someone was at the door and before I even turned my head to see, I knew who it was. My heart beat fast. I slowly turned to look, but the person had made his way over to me and my dad.

"I'll take care of her uncle," he said, putting his arm around me.

"Hey Aadhi," my dad said. "That's good. Do not listen to her. Ask her to stay here and please be with her."

"Don't worry, uncle," he said. "Rest assured I will take care of her. You please go ahead. You are needed there."

My father nodded and was about to leave when Aadhi held his hand tight. My dad understood in an instant the pain of the unspoken words.

"Hey," my dad said, pulling him into a hug. "Your father will be safe. I won't let anything happen to him. That's why I'm going."

Aadhi nodded.

It wasn't news that uncle Deva tended to get impulsive easily. Extremely impulsive. That too, at a time like this, he had to be overseen by someone pragmatic, with a calm mind—like my dad ... or like Aadhi.

That was when it struck me. Aadhi had actually left his impulsive, short- tempered father at a time like this ... for me. My eyes widened.

"Aadhi, you should go," I said. "I don't need to be taken care of. Deva uncle needs you right now more than me."

"He'll be fine," Aadhi said. "You're as impulsive and stupid as my dad. I'll watch you."

"Excuse me?"

Aadhi pulled me inside a room and closed the door behind him.

"Yeah," he yelled. "You're a miniature version of him. He always wants to stand up for others and doesn't give a damn about himself or his own. You're growing up to be just like him. Your father is the most stable and pragmatic man I've ever seen. Just like how you look up to my father, I look up to yours because he doesn't jeopardize his family for the sake of others and that's the way I'm growing up to be."

I was at a loss of words for one whole minute while he stood stiff, staring down at me like I was some mischievous kid. I'd never seen him so angry.

"The grass is always greener on the other side. Guess we have the wrong dads," I said and that made him smile. But only for a second.

"Look, Shravya," he said. "I'm scared."

"I know, Aadhi." I said and held his hands tight. "I'm scared, too. But there isn't a choice now but to face our fears. You know they need us. The victim's families need us."

"Oh, come on!" Aadhi pushed my hand away, cringed and got up. "You think I haven't heard these words before? I've heard the exact same tone and these words over and over again all my life. You're just like my dad. You'll never listen. You'll put us all in danger. I lost my mom over this attitude. I'm not ready to lose you, too!"

My chest flared in anger.

"You know your dad isn't responsible for your mom's death," I yelled. "And if I may recall, she was just like your dad too. It wasn't anyone's fault. It happened because it was meant to and I'm extremely sorry that it hurt you so bad and fucked up your life. You have my sympathy. But right now, there are dead people out there who died without knowing why. Their pieces are scattered out there like pieces of dung. Old and feeble fathers are forced to recognize their bodies. Do you realize the intensity of this situation?"

"I get that, Shravya," he said and moved towards me to hold me as I was shaking like a leaf. "Trust me, I do," he said. "But…"

"Stop right there," I said and pushed him away. "Don't you think their parents deserve a little respect and consolation at the least? Am I asking us to go out there and beat up the owner? No! I want us to be there with the victims' family and give them our useless shoulders." I paused for a deep breath. He didn't budge. "Seriously Aadhi, if you don't move your ass right now, you're not the man I know. And hey, please don't call yourself stable or pragmatic. Being stable comes with being strong. And you're definitely not pragmatic. Please don't compare yourself to my dad. He's actually stable because he's out there helping those in need while you're just a pathetic little boy who is too scared to help others because it might just end up hurting him. I'll tell you who you are. You're a frigging coward, Aadhi! A chicken. And do not, just do not blame your father for helping others just because you don't have the spine to do that, you selfish snob!"

Silence lingered for a minute.

Aadhi slumped on the bed, his head hung low, his eyes fixed on me. He did not say a word and I knew that I had pushed the buttons too hard. But that did not matter to me.

"I'm sorry," he said and his words came out muffled. I think I made him cry. "You're right. I'll get the bike. Let's go to Veera Explosives."

* * *

We took to the road without uttering another word. His familiar scent drifted towards me as he drove the bike and I swallowed hard, turning away. I had said some pretty hurtful things. I could have explained it to him in a calm way, but I hadn't. That was me. I fling my thoughts without a warning. Maybe that's why I don't have friends. Those who knew me and loved me enough to handle me, stayed. Others left and I didn't care.

After two minutes, we reached the lane that led to the factory—the one lane that uncle Deva always warned me to stay away from. Now I knew why. The road was eerily lonely—like some kind of a forbidden path. The feeling it gave was pure chills—literally and figuratively. Literally because the plants on the sides of the road were extremely green and untamed. The sides of the lane were overgrown with tall, dense herbs almost reaching out on the roads like green hands, about to get us. It might sound silly, but my heart leapt. I almost crushed Aadhi's shoulder in fear. He sensed it and picked up speed. I closed my eyes until he pulled to a halt.

I opened my eyes. Thank God, that lane had ended. I saw a bunch of people and beyond them were the bare concrete buildings. There was a red board that hung in front of the building. It said 'Veera Explosives'.

My stomach turned.

"Before we go," said Aadhi, "hold my hand, okay? Maybe this is cowardice. Maybe you think I don't have a spine. But pity me and hold my hand if poss—"

I grabbed his hand before he could complete that sentence. He sighed and held my hand tight.

Sirens wailed and people were running about here and there. The eerie feeling was back. We headed to the factory premises and the police stopped us in an instant. Aadhi pulled me behind him.

A short, stout, pot-bellied, paan-eating policeman stopped us.

"Kids not allowed here," he said. "Get out of here."

"We are with him," Aadhi pointed to Deva uncle who stood inside the factory with a group of people.

"I don't care," he said, his face blank, his mouth chewing continually, saliva forming at the corners of his mouth. "Clear out before things get ugly."

"Hey!" I said and moved towards him.

"It's okay," Aadhi said, tightening his grip on my hand. "We'll go."

"What?" I asked as we moved away. "I thought you said you weren't a coward."

"I did," Aadhi said, his eyes darting. "Doesn't mean we have to put up with these people. I know how to get us in there. Just trust me."

We moved away from the crowd and took to another lane that extended perpendicularly to that spooky lane. A smaller, warmer one, in fact. Not so eerily green like that lane. This one was dry and natural.

"There is another entrance to this factory," he said. "Back entrance. That's their weak spot. Less guarded, less accessible and well out of sight. If we can find it, we could get inside unnoticed."

I narrowed my eyes.

"How do you know so much about the factory?"

"You know..." he said and looked away. "Knowledge is a tricky thing."

"Did Deva uncle tell you?"

"Nah!" Aadhi said. We walked as the screeching of the two-wheeler would have drawn attention. The short, curvy path twisted and turned in front of us. It was clear that we were taking the shortcuts to go around the premises and pretty soon, we would reach the back entrance.

"Don't lie. Only he could have told you."

"No way," Aadhi said. "My dad is too much of a straight arrow to even think about shortcuts."

I froze.

"So..." I said and paused. "You learnt this by yourself."

"Yep."

"Just in case things went south," I said.

"Yep."

"To help your dad out. In case he gets into a soup like this."

"Well said," Aadhi said as he asked me to crouch as we heard footsteps. "That's very perceptive of you."

"What? Asking you to crouch?"

"No. Planning ahead to stand with your father. But why Veera Explosives? How did you figure you'd be needing this route?"

"Those guys are dangerous and well-connected. Dad was always getting into a beef with them. I knew it was only a matter of time before they would react. But I never expected something like this."

We heard footsteps. A farmer passed by us with a sickle and disappeared into the paddy field. After making sure he was well out of sight, we got up and moved towards the building. We could see the splinters from the rods everywhere. A thought struck me and I could feel my eyes widen.

"Do you think..." I paused as my head palpitated before I could even say it.

"Think what?"

"Do you think this was intentional? This blast."

"Thing is," Aadhi contemplated, "we will never know."

* * *

The back side of the factory was completely dry, unlike its front, which was the one of the greenest parts of Achipatti. We pushed away the dried grass and almost crawled towards the building. There was a broken wall in front of us. Just a small opening. Maybe there had been a minor blast before that. We had to tuck our stomachs in to enter, but our backs got hurt by the crevices. The factory was located on land that was a few metres below the surrounding area. Maybe that's why the effect of the blast had been disastrous. There was no place to spread or scatter the effect.

The buildings looked very feeble and unprotected for an explosives factory. At the farthest end, on the right side of the front entrance, we could see a number of lorries standing—probably the ones that brought chemical supplies and machines into the factory. After an excruciating struggle with the crevice on the wall, we were finally in. Uncle Deva, the police, and a few other people were visible now. Thick, tall grass covered us, and Aadhi was right. No one could see us.

"Now what do we do?" I asked.

"We go near them and we eavesdrop. That's it. We get to know what's happening without getting kicked out."

I nodded and together, we stealthily made our way towards uncle Deva, without making any significant movement apart from our walk. As soon as we reached the building, we crouched behind it. We could faintly hear the voices.

"We should go by that blue building." Aadhi whispered, pointing to the building in front of us. "Only then we'd be able to hear what they are saying."

"But it's risky."

"I'm going. Come with me if you want to."

With that, he started moving slowly towards the blue building. I could see what was making him do all this; calling him a coward must have certainly sent his blood rushing. I felt sorry for him and I wished he knew I had not meant it. I followed him, and soon enough, we were able to clearly hear the conversation.

First of all, I laid my eyes on the blasted building which was on our right, a few metres in front of us. The rods of the building were exposed, and they looked haphazard, like fried hair. The façade was completely gone and just when I was checking out the ground; I noticed some crimson red mass lying indiscriminately in the mud. Near the mass lay something brown—like a soft piece of rattan. No…some finger-like projections protruded from it.

Toes!

That was a goddamn severed foot.

My eyes widened.

I huddled close to Aadhi, grabbed his shoulder and pointed to it.

"Wh…what is that?" I asked.

He instantly pulled my head away towards him.

"Don't look," he said.

Tears started rolling effortlessly. "This is all so bad," I said, crying. "This is inhuman. Why is *that* lying like a piece of dog shit over there?"

"Shush," Aadhi said, holding me tight. "I know. It's horrible. But we have to listen to them."

I quietened down and concentrated on the conversation. I could clearly hear uncle Deva yelling at the police. My dad stood near him.

"This is not how you speak, Mr Rajendran," uncle Deva said to a man in khaki, whose cap was utterly dirty. "We do not know the number. It's beyond twenty, I'm sure. And more bodies are stuck beneath the debris. We have to take them out."

"I'm not sure that's the case here," said dirty-cap. "Mr Vijay denies any sort of accusation like this. He…"

"Bite me," uncle Deva interrupted, moving an inch closer to the police. "Like that schmuck Vijay knows shit."

"Mind your words, Mr Deva. We'd be happy to take you behind bars," dirty-caps said.

"Do that first. Let's see who takes who," Deva uncle pulled the *kaapu* on his hand back and urged the police to raise a hand at him, so that he could put his fist into dirty-caps' face.

Aadhi sighed near me.

"See?" he pointed. "Is this pragmatic? His anger always clouds his senses."

"His anger is reasonable. Anyone would react the same way."

"But going to jail isn't going to help anyone!" said Aadhi.

I nodded. He was making sense.

"Deva, calm down," I heard my dad say and grab Deva uncle's hand tight. "Mr Rajendran," he turned to the police. "Deva is speaking on behalf of the villagers and his anger is justified. He has the right and grit to stand for his own people. And today he has lost those people he stood for. That deserves some respect and accountability from you, or anyone else for that matter. So, I suggest you consider treating this man with respect before you side with cold, heartless people who are bribing you."

Dirty cap's jaw dropped open.

"See?" Aadhi told me, with a glint in his eyes. "Now that's heroic and pragmatic. Understand why I look up to him?"

I nodded, my head low.

In an instant, I felt Aadhi jump beside me.

"I have an idea," he said with a start. He picked out his mobile and dialled a number. I did not read the name on the screen.

"Who is it?" I said, and he shushed me.

"Hello sir, this is Aadhi. I need your help."

13
BOINKED

Archana

TEN YEARS AGO...

Something didn't fit.

It seemed too good to be true. Frankly, I had involved myself in this only for him. I had no interest in nailing a normal corporate company that had no worse intentions than any other company who wanted to earn profits. The tattooed guy was bad news indeed; but I checked out every corporate event. They all had someone like the tattoo-man watching over them. Guess it was just a normal thing every big guy does. I bet I had exaggerated about him being an executor because I so badly wanted to see something wrong in them. For him.

Deep down, I knew Deva's obsession with this one company, just because it was in his own village, was pointless. I knew I would find no dirt on them apart from what one would usually find on any company that was growing big. But now, when I was squinting my eyes on the screen, a knot tightened in my stomach. It grew and grew without reason and reached the pit of my throat. My assumptions, my careless attitude towards Veera Explosives, were all fading out.

Like I said, something did not fit.

It was two in the morning and I was up in my bedroom, sitting on the thin mattress on my feeble cot. My parents slept in their room or sometimes in the hall. Like I said, our house is really small and simple. I liked to be up at night, reading up or watching true crime documentaries, gearing up punchy arguments in my head to nail those bastards. Pardon the swag here, but sometimes the arguments I craft in my head, picturing myself in a courtroom, are so crisp, gasp-worthy and funny at the same time! I could make the guilty one slither first, wither later and disappear slowly with my cut-throat, yet insanely punchy words. I knew I had that in me.

I knew I could have pursued Science. Maybe it was the unsaid bloodlust in me, the urge to find the wrong in everything, and most importantly, the hatred for people in general, that made me pick up law.

My throat closed as I watched it—the video that my friend and mentor, Nikitha Krishnan, had sent me via email.

A video of the man I saw in the shiny purple shirt getting into a fistfight with the handsome Vijay Kumar I saw a few days ago. Hard punches by the fat fist on the toned, yet meek chest of Vijay. Harder ones on the face. It was brutal. Why was Gunasekaran mercilessly beating the crap out of Vijay? And why was nobody stopping him?

Someone on the inside had filmed it and somehow, my sneaky mentor had got access to it. This was huge.

The video had no sound.

I called her.

"Girl, don't ask me what's the reason behind that ugly fist fight," Nikitha said.

"Uh, hello to you too," I said.

"You know my sources."

"I do. I don't question how you got access to it. I just want some more detail."

Nikitha had her ways with the system. She worked in the Coimbatore District Court—she was one of the star lawyers, indeed. Not a very legal, *lawful* lawyer, though. To put it blatantly, she was the most illegal lawyer one could find. She did not care about good or bad. If you want dirt, she will dig it right up and offer it on the platter. If you want the guilty to be released, she would turn the case around and blame the victim to an extent that they wished they had been the guilty one. Basically, she was heartless, ruthless and extremely good at her job. Criminals loved her. They hired her because they knew she would save all of their asses with her sharp words and sharper mind.

You see, I wasn't like her. I had a heart, not for people, but for the truth. I chose her as my mentor because I wanted to learn her ways, but wanted to swing by the truth, unlike her.

Unlawful ways to get justice. What's wrong with that?

I had just asked her to dig up dirt on Veera Explosives. She would do anything I asked, because well, if there was one thing she adored, it was talent. Not goodness, not people; just pure, unhindered talent. She saw that in me. She hated my quest for right and truth, but loved the desperate urge in me to make it big.

She had her sources. No one knew how or where or who gave them to her. She just had them.

"No details, babe." Nikitha said in her boyish tone. I could hear her chewing. "Fat guy just boinked the cute one."

"Where did this happen?"

"In Gunasekaran's home. Vijay went there for something and got beaten up."

"Why? Why do you think he went there?" I asked her.

"Honestly?" she chewed more. "Partners of a big corporation in a brawl. What do you think that is?"

"Betrayal. Money."

"There you go. The cute one might have cheated the fat one on some financial deal. Must have learnt from his father."

"What do you mean?" I asked.

"Really? You don't know?" she squealed. "His father, Jagan Kumar, was a big-time fraud in the name of a philanthropist. Robbed the government of funds for his fake NGOs that channelled money. Died of cancer. Karma, the best judge."

"Oh!" I said. The information was too much to process.

"If you want to nail the cute guy, I suggest you go after the fat one," Nikitha said.

"Hmm."

"Also," she said, her boyish voice now low. "How's your crush? Deva, right? Man, he looks so hot! You know, if you're into the manly, elderly look."

My eyes brightened. "Yes."

"I'mma be straight with you," she said, "He's a real man. I have come across a lot of good people and I can easily dig up dirt on them. Believe me."

"Oh yeah, I believe you on that."

"But this one," she paused to chew, "A real star. He genuinely wants to help people. Doesn't expect credit for that at all. Prefers to stay hidden. That's the wow factor.

"How?"

"In times when the mere act of buying food for a beggar is shot and made viral for people to appreciate, he does so many things and prefers to stay anonymous. He had to be persuaded a lot to accept the awards that he has received."

I chuckled. She sighed.

"I tell you. I found no dirt on him at all! Nothing. Nil. Nada!" She said, emphasizing each word. "He's quite a catch."

"That's something." I said, shutting my eyes in happiness. Nikitha appreciating someone? I did not need any better assurance.

"Don't do anything stupid for him," she said and hung up the phone.

I sat there, devoid of thoughts. I checked the time. It was three in the morning. I was thinking about the video and pacing around in the room. It would be a long time before Deva would wake up. What should I do?

One weird thought occurred in my head and freaked the hell out of me. Adrenaline surged its way up from my stomach to my nostrils. It was crazy, but I knew I was going to do it.

I changed my clothes, packed my laptop, and headed out of the house to the bus stand, which was a few metres away. By bus stand, I mean just a hut in front of an open space. The cold morning air felt nice and eerie. The only street light in the village was dim and flickering. The lack of sleep was finding its way up, but I blinked it away. Soon enough, I spotted a bus I wanted to get on.

The bus said 'Coimbatore North'.

14
CLAIRVOYANT IN CHAOS

1 December 2016
Achipatti Village

It took about two hours, and we were stranded there without food or water. The conversations between the police and the people were driving us insane. The more they talked, the more punches we took in our guts. The details of the incident were pretty clear by then.

At about midnight, some sort of distress alarm had sounded in a machine in the blasted building. Few workers had gone in to check it. Before they could do something about it, the machine had exploded, blasting the whole building and killing the people in it. The blast had been so intense that the concrete blocks from the building were thrown to a distance of five kilometres. As I had guessed, since the factory was located a few metres below the ground, the effect of the blast had multiplied. The building had shifted from the intensity and had fallen inside the premises instead of splattering out.

The saddest thing was that the workers were trapped inside and were splattered during the blast, their flesh lying all over the place.

By that time, we had exited the way we came in and had reached our bike.

"Nobody deserves this. Even the worst person in the world. This is just insane," I said to Aadhi.

"Yes ... but it happened. We have to look ahead instead of drowning in this pain. It's easier to drown but harder to try to swim to stay on top. What do you want to do?"

"I'd like my chances to stay on top."

"Good," Aadhi said. "Then stay with me. Stay focussed on what we'd do next."

"Okay. I will. Who was it that you called? Some VIP? A friend? A mentor?"

"An apt combination of all three."

A white Honda city whooshed to a halt in front of us. The driver got out and ran to open the passenger door. Out came a short, elderly man with typical old man's sandals. He had stern eyes, thin lips, but a surprisingly blank countenance. His shoulders were broad and stiff and he had a potbelly. He wore a crisp white oxford shirt whose sleeves hung about free, and neatly pressed black pants. His hair was long, slick, and combed back. A typical outlook of a well-educated elderly Tamil man whom the kids feared, and the people respected. So naturally, I feared the man.

Aadhi held out his hand, but the man pulled him in for a tight hug.

"I'm sorry," he said, squeezing his hand. His voice, unlike his stern countenance, was softer and a bit high-pitched.

"Shravya," Aadhi pointed to me after pulling away from the hug. "This is Advocate Madhav Kumar from Trichy. He is literally the best in urgent cases like these."

"Hello sir," I held out my hand and he shook it. "How are you related to him?" I asked Aadhi.

"He is my guru. My mentor since when I was a child."

"You still didn't answer my question," I said.

"I'll answer that," said the lawyer. "I'm his mother's elder brother. Aadhi's uncle."

* * *

The three of us sat down at the village tea shop, a little further away from the factory. We weren't in the mood to drink tea or eat anything. We both had just downed a few glasses of water, but Mr Madhav Kumar ordered a special tea and three masala bondas. As soon as they arrived, he polished them away in a jiffy. I wondered how the man could eat this much at a time like this. It felt a bit ghoulish even if he was peckish.

Was he even good at his job? I highly doubted. But I trusted Aadhi and was curious to see how things turned out.

"Pollachi police on scene?" he asked, eating the bonda.

"Yes sir," Aadhi replied.

"Rajendran is a sensible man. He'll help us. Put Deva in touch with him."

Aadhi and I looked at each other. I rolled my eyes.

"What?" Mr Madhav Kumar asked as his eyes narrowed. "No way. Don't tell me he got into a beef with him already."

I knew in that instant that he didn't like uncle Deva. Probably he still blamed him for his sister's death.

"Pretty much," Aadhi said and guffawed.

"Mr Rajendran was conniving," I said, staring at Aadhi for not defending his father. "Anyone would have done the same. If I must say, uncle Deva was *actually* being nice to that man. If it were me, things would have been different."

Both the men were silent. The lawyer had even stopped chewing.

"A mini Deva, I presume," he chewed again. He then turned to Aadhi. "No wonder you run about with her."

I could feel the blood rushing to my ears. Aadhi held my hand and squeezed it. I took the hint and pursed my lips.

"I've got it," Mr Madhav Kumar said. "We'll figure it out."

"But uh..." Aadhi said.

"I sense you're about to talk about Vijay."

"Yes. What are we going to do about him? Can we talk?"

"Oh, he's a man who doesn't like to be disturbed with details. What's he saying to the police about the blast?"

"That it was an accident. That the machine was at fault and the worker had mishandled it."

"Negligence, my foot," the lawyer said, relishing the last bite of his second bonda. "People were blasted to an unidentifiable pulp; counts as murder nonetheless."

I wondered how the man could activate his appetite whilst talking about gruesome things. I think the people who work with crime their entire lives somehow get used to it to an extent that it becomes a part of their daily conversation—like how we talk about movies and stuff.

"Will we be able to get him?" asked Aadhi.

"Tough. But we'll try our best. Meanwhile, ask Deva to play nice. His behaviour shouldn't cost us." He paused. "Once more."

"He is a great man," I said, detaching myself from Aadhi's squeeze. "uncle Deva, I mean. I'm really sorry that your beloved sister passed away. Really. But you're wrong to think uncle Deva did not treat your sister well. Truth is, he is a hero. Your sister would have been proud of him, I'm sure of that. She would agree with me if she were alive today. Stop blaming him for everything that went wrong. It's not true."

Silence.

Aadhi's mouth dropped open, and so did Mr Madhav Kumar's. I knew I had crossed the limit, but so be it. It had to come out some day. I was tired of everyone blaming uncle Deva. My chest fumed with pride. I could see the torn bonda inside his open mouth. His eyes teared up a bit. In anger or sadness, I didn't know. I didn't care. His body jolted a bit, and he moved a tad to the left as he blinked. He was an old man—intelligent, but feeble; and the raw, stinging words from my mouth were a blow to him. For a second, I felt bad. But uncle Deva's face flashed in front of my eyes. I didn't feel bad anymore for anyone who thought any less of him.

Madhav Kumar got up, placed the money on the counter with his trembling hands, and trod jerkily towards his car. Something still pushed him to the left, as if he was falling. He managed to sit inside. I could see him through the glass. He was crying.

"You're crazy," Aadhi yelled with his eyes wide.

"You are the crazy one to put up with someone who looks down upon your dad," I screamed. "Sir, my ass."

The Honda drove away.

"Look. He's the best at his job. He is known for helping out people at times like this. If there is one person who could help us come out of this, it's him."

I contemplated his words. I felt nothing.

A wail of sirens broke my chain of thoughts. A media van swished past us and screeched to a halt a few metres away. There were loud footsteps, screams and scuttling as if people were running about in confusion.

"Oh no!" sighed Aadhi and pressed his head on his palm. "I knew it! I knew he would do something like this. Dad!" he ground his teeth.

"What do you mean? Is he okay?" My heart picked up pace.

"Yeah, yeah," Aadhi said. "Let's go."

* * *

We reached the factory in the next two minutes. It was filled with people—one set moving about in confusion and the other set slowly settling down in front of a platform like set up. A few men were hurriedly arranging it.

"A stage?" I asked. "What's going on?"

"Another one of your uncle's stupid moves."

"Shut it," I said, and Aadhi ignored me. He pulled my hand and walked towards the stage.

"Anna!" he said to one of the men arranging the stage. "Where is appa?"

"He is busy, thambi," the man said, wiping his sweat. "He has to speak to these people."

Aadhi nodded and headed directly inside the factory. The police tried to stop him, but to no use. The crowd slowly grew massive and the police, instead of trying to stop them, had to protect them. Deva uncle stood a few yards away from us, talking to the police and a few people who were his disciples.

Deva uncle's sullen face brightened as soon as he laid his eyes on his son.

"Aadhi," he said. "Come join me. And please drop Shravya at home. This is not the place for her."

"Bet it's not," I said and frowned.

Uncle Deva almost hugged his son, but Aadhi pushed him away. "You're getting yourself into grave trouble. Please don't do this. The police have their eyes on you." He paused and grabbed his father's arm. "Dad, I'm afraid."

"Son," Deva uncle's voice was calm. "If I don't do this, then who will?"

With that, he grabbed the rusted, blue-coloured horn speaker from one of his disciples and headed to the stage.

We followed him. Aadhi's grip on my hand was turning tighter and painful.

The families of the victims occupied the foot of the stage. They wept and wept, a sound I still struggle to forget. People from the other villages hugged them and consoled them, while some cried along with them. The coming together of the suffering families somehow seemed to have a warm effect on them. I knew Deva uncle would have made the right decision. My heart swelled with pride and I removed Aadhi's tight grip on my hand.

"We should support him," I said. "I know I'm going to."

Uncle Deva sprinted up on the stage and faced the crowd.

Everyone fell silent. You could have heard a pin drop.

The families stopped weeping, the confusion halted, and the police refrained from moving. The silence lasted only for a second, though.

After that, the crying and howling increased, while some of his ardent fans clapped with their full might.

Various voices said different things.

"Save us, anna!"

"Anna, please kill Vijay!"

"Only you can save us, anna!"

"Only after seeing you, I feel alive."

Uncle Deva swallowed, then pulled the horn speaker to his mouth and spoke.

"I'm sure you have an idea why we have gathered here. What has happened here is inhuman and brutal and my heart burns with rage," he wiped his tears, but the crowd made no noise. They listened to him with the utmost concentration. "What can we do, brothers and sisters? Should we fight against them or mourn the loss of our dear ones? Should we fight back or chicken out?"

"Fight back!!!"

The factory resounded with their energy.

"To do that correctly, we have to be patient first. We have to let the legal system handle this with our support. If they don't do it correctly..." he said, bit his lips, slowly shook his head and gave a fiery stare at the police officers and held eye contact with them, his face burning with rage.

I was in awe. This was just like the movies and I got goosebumps and chills all over. Not just me. The crowd cheered with emotion, like they cheered an on-screen hero.

This was an unsaid but direct threat from an unarmed, simple man to the revolver-carrying officers of the law! And all they could do was just look at him in shock, terror and some admiration, especially from the rare, honest officers.

"However big or rich or untouchable they are, they would have to face my wrath. Well, especially then. I know not of the rich's power! All I know is that I would go to any extent to get justice for my loved ones."

His eyes turned crimson. He climbed down the stage and I couldn't hold myself back. I just ran and hugged him. I thought I hugged him because he needed it, but deep down, I knew I was the one in need.

"You're awesome, uncle," I said. "I'm sure you will win this fight."

He held me as he pulled the horn speaker close to his mouth. "I don't want victory," he said. "I just want justice."

* * *

The protests lasted for a week. For the entire week, we would go home late at night, sleep and come back early in the morning to help the protestors. Though Aadhi hated every bit of what was taking place under the instruction of his father, he was the one who took the best care of the protestors. He arranged for food, juices, buttermilk and even chocolates to lift their moods.

The news slowly grew bigger and a lot of people from the nearby villages began to join. The sensible, practical people joined because the water had completely gotten polluted because of the factory and the emotional, sensitive ones joined because they were sad for the victims.

So naturally, it was a win-win. Every single person was attracted to the protest.

The protest grew so rapidly that soon enough, the media people stormed the place like vultures. The Hindu, Times of India, Times Now, a few famous local channels—everyone covered the news. The locals were interviewed, and they all spoke about Vijay Kumar's duplicity—how the water got polluted and how the factory had ruined everything that this village held dear.

When they were asked how they had made this protest into a revolution, they mentioned uncle Deva's name with a glint in their eyes.

"He is our everything," said a man, grabbing the mic from the reporter. "Without him, we couldn't even dream of raising our voices against Vijay."

When the media guys wanted to interview uncle Deva, he was nowhere to be seen. Everyone knew he hated the fame or attention he got out of something he did for a cause. His picture was released to the media by someone, though he hated it.

His dark complexion, bright smile, deep eyes, ruffled hair and the scar on the left temple certainly popped out on screen and he looked so handsome.

The blast case got transferred to Coimbatore Police as the protests drew a lot more attention than expected. The police now had to handle this case with care, as there were powerful eyes on it.

"Everything is going according to plan," I said as we stood back from the media, rested our tired backs on a tree trunk and drank buttermilk.

"Never say that," Aadhi said. "Till now he hasn't made a move.

"Who? Vijay?"

"Yep."

"And that affects you?"

"Yes."

"But that's good, right?" I said. "Maybe he's scared."

"That's the thing. He never gets scared." Aadhi said. "Ever."

"Now I understand why both of you look so sad, even if things are going according to our plan. You don't know what Vijay's going to do."

"Yes."

"He can't be that bad. He seemed like a harmless man. If Deva uncle gives one punch to his gut, he'll crack like an eggshell."

Aadhi gave a wry smile. "You don't know him. At all."

"But you two do, right? You know him well. Then why are you guys scared?"

"That's because," Aadhi said and paused, "we know him *too* well."

15
Murder? The Worst Crime? Well, Here Comes Betrayal

Archana

TEN YEARS AGO...

It was a two-hour drive to Coimbatore North. There wasn't a direct route, so I had to change two buses. By the time I had my morning coffee and sat down at the second bus stand for an hour contemplating the arguments in my head, daylight broke. It did not take me long to find Gunasekaran's house. It was a three-storied bungalow in the interior of the city. It did not look even a tad like a rowdy's house. Wait a second. How was it supposed to be? A sludge in a slum?

Gunasekaran's house was the embodiment of the phrase -'spick and span'. The rugged exteriors with no dirt, the large, shiny gate, the freshly watered areca palms with no dust on the leaves and the neat crispy lawn recently mowed with water droplets on their tips—this place was a dream. I stood outside the gate. A security guard came out irritated, but thought differently the instant he saw me. He gazed at me up and down, his mouth slightly open.

"I'm here to see Gunasekaran," I said.

"One moment," he said. "I'll let ayya know."

Woah!

Ayya? Really?

Fancy calling the head bumper that.

My instinct told me to call Deva and let him know what was happening. But frankly, the reason I was here was to impress him. Partners falling out, that too this dramatically, was a textbook opportunity to make our move against the corporation. Only, I wanted to make it without involving him, so that he could see how wonderful I was. Not just that. As a lawyer, I thought I could take it into my own hands and I needed this on-field experience to practice my argumentative skills.

Something told me this would either be my boldest achievement or my biggest mistake. It would just take moments to find out.

"You can go in," the security guard interrupted my thoughts.

"Ayya in there, uh, buddy?" I grinned at him. He became red with embarrassment. He grinned back, his shoulders lifting in shyness.

I walked inside the bungalow, every step making my jaw drop open, owing to its immaculate beauty. This was straight out of the *Inside Outside* magazine. I had little idea about architecture, but I could tell immediately that the house was a seamless mixture of post modernism and baroque architecture with a tinge of minimalism. Baroque, known for its heaviness and grandeur and minimalism, with plain colours and nothingness—total opposites mixed together in haphazard order creating harmony instead of chaos.

Even a rich artist wouldn't have a house as beautiful and classy as this. I entered the massive living room with French windows that connected the floor and ceiling, ensuring visual connectivity. On the sofa, at some distance, sat Gunasekaran in a shiny orange shirt, the sun from the windows glaring off his shirt.

I walked confidently the moment an icicle of fear tickled my gut, just to cover it up. His sagged face brightened the instant he saw me. I was glad I had that effect on men.

"Well, Allo there!" he cooed. His voice, somehow, was exactly how I imagined it. Hoarse and fat just like his body. "Who are you and what is your name?"

"Hello sir, I mean, ayya," I said with a smile. Yes, the killer smile I was known for. His jaws dropped open. I sat down opposite him. "My name is Archana, and I'm from Achipatti village."

"You're so damn pretty," he said. Yeah, just like that. His directness scared me a little.

"Thanks, I guess."

"Let's get you some water. You want juice, snacks?"

"Just water is cool," I said and nodded at the servant, who came sprinting with his hands folded.

"Ma'am," he bowed. My chest flared up. Woah! Goons were awesome.

"Tell me, Ms Archana," started Gunasekaran. "What brings you here?"

"I'm a law graduate, well, a lawyer. I have been looking into Veera Explosives and its owner, Vijay Kumar."

"Vijay is not the owner," he gritted his teeth.

"Fair enough. You are!"

"Damn right I am." He banged his fist on the teapoy. That was when I noticed. This man had frigging Zaha Hadid's water table as his teapoy. And he was ready to crack it. This design had rocked the world. Oh boy! I did not want the limited edition marvel to crack under this man's fat fist that would break anything.

"Calm down, sir. Your anger is understandable. In fact, that's exactly why I'm here. I could offer something that would help your vengeance find a more legal way of expressing itself."

His eyes narrowed. "What do you mean?"

"Like I said, I'm a lawyer," I said and pulled my laptop out. I switched it on and played the million-dollar video. "Ouch," I said when the fist landed flat on Vijay's face. "That must have hurt. But it's not enough. If I was you, I would have made his face crack."

His breaths turned jerky, making his saggy chest go up and down. His evil smile emerged. "Really?"

"I know you hate him," I said, throwing a smile, "So do I."

He looked at me, his face turning thoughtful. "Why?"

"I have my reasons," I said, "The factory is polluting my village. I want it gone."

"Fair enough."

"I want you to tell me what Vijay did to you that made you punch him. We both can nail him down legally. He will be put away for years."

"You mean in prison?" he asked, his face curious and happy.

"Yes!"

"How do I trust this isn't a setup? That son of a bitch would go to any extent to fuck with me. Sending a pretty chick to make me speak is the first thing he'd do. To get revenge."

"Look at this," I said and showed him my presentation against Veera Explosives. "I have been working on this for months. And this is my birth certificate. See where I hail from? Achipatti. I care only about my village. These guys are messing it up. As a lawyer, and an educated being," I said and paused, "don't you think I would want to nail that son of a bitch?"

He gazed at me, his face turning gentle. He heaved a sigh and got comfortable on the sofa. He trusted me. He was going to open up. My heart paced. This was working.

"He cut me out," said Gunasekaran. "Sold my partnership off to another explosives company who wanted to collaborate with him." He bent forward. His pot belly stopped him, but he tried more. I bent too.

"The Achipatti factory is a game changer," he whispered. "The water there is going to increase the produce several-fold. We have customers lined up abroad, too. Big guys. Ready to throw money for the quality of explosives. You know who got those customers?"

"I'm betting on you." I smiled. He gave a saggy smile back. The eyes stayed evil.

"The money would have changed everything. Right when things were about to get bigger, I knew about the fuck up. He used me and threw me away. Came here to peacefully let me know that I was out. You think I'd go for it?"

"Hell no!"

"Exactly! So, I jammed his head. That son of a bitch!"

"Wow. This is amazing," I said. "This could put him away for life. And the factory would be easily removed from the village," I said and thought. "Wait a second. You don't have a problem now because you're out, right?"

He laughed. "Yes. I'd help you remove the factory. Anything to burn his ass..."

Ass burning? Really? Deva said that often. I imagined his face when I told him this! That excitement on his handsome face. I couldn't help but smile.

"I need the details from you, sir," I said, "to make it work. Details of the customers, the proof of collaboration with the other explosive company, everything."

"I know what all a lawyer needs. I'll have that sent to you," he smiled, "You seem like a little girl, but you're smart."

"That I am."

"You better be. If you mess this up," he said and shrugged. I got it. With this man's track record, I'd be long gone.

"I better don't," I said and got up. "I'll see myself out."

He got my contact number before I left. I headed out into the open and felt the sun on my face. It felt extremely good. See? It wasn't so hard at all. I pulled out my worn out mobile and dialled Deva's number. He picked up on the third ring.

"Deva, you won't believe what happened," I said.

"What? Where are you?" His voice sounded sleepy and heavy. I closed my eyes and let it linger. If this wasn't love, what was?

"I'm in Coimbatore North. I came here to meet Gunasekaran."

A pause. A jerky exhale. "What?" he screamed, panting hard. "Archana, what the hell? Why did you go without me? Are you crazy? Get out of there! I'm on my way. What the hell were you thinking?"

"It's not what you think," I cooed. "I have some big news."

"Nothing matters. You hear me? Nothing matters to me. Just get out of there. Fuck! Shit!" I heard a thud. I wondered if he fell out of bed or dropped his cell. Either way, I was happy. "I'm on my way," he said and hung up.

Nothing mattered to him when it came to my safety. That was new. He cared about me. Sweet. I threw a smile at the security guard and he jolted in shyness. Men!

The very thought that he was on his way for me filled me with ecstasy. I was falling in love with him and I could physically feel it, like a long, hot shower on a cold winter night. I smiled to myself.

I had nowhere else to go. This city seemed like a good place to spend some quality time with Deva. Let him freak out and come here. I'd give him the big news and probably, we'd hang out in a nice, posh restaurant for the day, instead of the hills and cowsheds and fields, which were also kind of nice. However, for once, I had to hang out with him like a lawyer on duty. *Lawyer.*

My mind rushed. Gunasekaran said that he *knew* what a lawyer needs. If so, why didn't he hire a lawyer against Vijay till now? Why suddenly believe in an amateur like me? Hell, why would he even trust me? With his money and connections, he could have hired the best lawyer to do this job for him. But he didn't. Why? I felt something jab into my heart and rip it apart. This was a trap. My head twirled. Something was horribly wrong. I couldn't figure it out. It didn't matter. I sprinted towards the gate.

"Not so soon," I heard Gunasekaran's voice from behind. I shut my eyes tight. Slowly, I turned to look at him, my legs not stopping. I was headed towards the gate as I saw five thugs who looked bigger than him emerge from the sides with guns in their hands.

This house was located in a desolate spot. I knew I couldn't make it out in time.

"You're the one helping Deva, right?" he asked with the same smile

I had seen in the picture, the eyes pure evil. My breath got caught in my throat. A dull tremor ran through me.

"What?" I said. "No."

I saw it all in a jiffy. They had all been eyeing Deva for a long while—tracking his every move and action. Deva, who was used to going to the site to curse, had suddenly stopped because I had asked him to stay calm. They had smelt something fishy. His silence bothered them. His lack of agitation made them uncomfortable. They were worried he was up to something. And when I started asking around in the lawyers' circle about Veera Explosives, someone from inside must have told them. There were rats inside every field. Just a little background check on me and where I hail from would have told them that I might be involved. Just to make sure, they had crafted a video and circled it amongst the lawyers, knowing that someone or the other would give it to me. It was all an act. The fist in the face, the fight, the story. All lies.

It was a trap. A ruse. It was all a setup to lure me out. To lure Deva out. And I fell for it. A tear escaped my eye.

"You think I'd snitch on Vijay? Hell, I'll die for him."

"You L-liar," I said, controlling my tears.

The smile was gone from his face, and his eyes stayed the same. The thugs beside him were getting worked up. I was no longer scared.

"You're too smart for this world. You'd bring us down. Especially if you're helping that nutcase, Deva. He won't stop. He will always be a threat to us, that righteous jerk. . ."

"Yes, he is. He won't stop, you money-minded prickheads! He will get you all. And you will rot in jail." I couldn't stop. I had pulled the wrong string. He gazed at the thugs. They sprinted towards me. I knew I had no chance, but I didn't want to die without a fight. I turned away from them and sprinted towards the gate. Thanks to the drooling security, it was luckily open.

I ran.

16
DESPERATE DESPERADO

4 December 2016
Kotagiri Hill, Coimbatore

The chill from the glass seemed to be seeping into the skin. The steaming hot water from the hot tub and the ice-cold scotch in his hand ceased him from relishing both, keeping him in his senses.

When one thinks about the hill stations in Tamil Nadu, only Ooty and Kodaikanal immediately pop up into the mind. However, there are certain simpler, more beautiful, smaller hills that remain lesser known and almost undisturbed by humans. Kotagiri—an enrapturing, yet duly underrated hill station was a dream. Tasteful people who had a knack for peace and loathed what other people generally loved knew the value of this place. Only a person with extreme peace in their head - one who is actually rich in mind - could fully enjoy the nothingness, the simplicity. Whereas someone simple or dull at heart needed the grandeur from outside to feel good about himself.

He was proud of the things he had done here, especially in the woods. He always felt at peace. Not just now, but since his childhood.

Born in a rich family, with his dad being the head of an industrial conglomerate, never once did he dream of taking his money or living under his roof. He knew he was going to strike out and make it on his own. The pinnacle was where he belonged. It didn't take long for him to change his life, step out of the rich mess, and slowly build an empire for himself. There was excessive grandeur around him, and he craved for excessive simplicity to balance the scale. He wanted to start off simple, take simple steps and create a fort for himself that gave him peace; or like others, crafted just for a show off. He desired his victory to evoke peace within himself and not chaos.

Kotagiri was devoid of dull-witted humans loitering around with no sense of direction, devoid of idiots who used the cold to have sex, devoid of tourists who dumped their self-induced trauma onto the hill thus wrecking the purity of the place, but was filled with animals and birds and insects that had better sense and intelligence than humans—the only ones that truly deserved the place.

This was the place for him. He rarely used the bungalow in Coimbatore. The chaos did not let him think. A random drive towards the Western Ghats to clear his head had found him in this place and he had immediately wanted it. He built a private villa in the most secluded part of the hill. Sprawled on an acre, it housed a big pool, a library and a big empty space with black walls and a large screen.

He took another sip, his eyes fixated on the gurgling water in the tub, lit from underneath. The smell of eucalyptus, usually intoxicating, suffocated him a tad today. Everything seemed that way. The drink in his hand, the hot water, the silence—everything. He blinked, not sure after how long, finished the drink and relaxed his numb muscles to climb out of the water.

Grabbing the towel from the sunlounger, he wrapped it around his waist and moved towards the dimly-lit villa. The marble floors, the slender columns, the simple yet grand architecture were confusing him today. He headed straight to the room with the black walls. The 'Thinking Room' as he liked to call it. The large screen usually stayed empty, because all the calculations and plans were done in his head. Only when something was unfathomable and bugged his mind, he loaded the notes and images on the screen and stared at them for hours, sitting on his beanbag.

Today there were no notes. No scribblings. No chaos to draw out a solution from. No question that needed an answer. Just one big picture on the entire screen—the picture of a man with a dark complexion, deep eyes, ruffled hair and a noticeable scar on his left temple.

He stared at it for an hour without even the slightest movement. Just a dark stare. He then got up and headed to his cabin and collapsed on the executive chair, heaving a deep sigh.

His office was entirely dark—grey walls, dark curtains, mahogany table and chairs, a black wall clock that did not work and a black and silver nameplate in front of him that said:

VIJAY KUMAR
Chairman, Veera Explosives

Somehow the sight of it did not inspire a stroke of glory like it usually did. His gaze moved to the dark photograph in front of him. The photograph that he saw every day before he sat at work, before he slept and after he woke up. The photograph that pushed him to the edge of sanity, but kept him at it.

It was a group photo of a happy family celebrating Pongal. In the middle stood the same man that was on the big screen a while ago. The man had his arms around a teenage boy and a girl. And there was a big smile on his face.

A smile! How can *he* smile?

Though the smile just sent shivers down his back every day, today he just couldn't take it. He threw the scotch glass across the room. It smashed into a million pieces, the sound of it hanging in the air for a minute. He clenched his teeth and pulled the photograph towards him. He grabbed a CD marker pen from the stand, threw the lid and drew an X on the man's face.

He marked it with so much force that the nib broke and the whole face in the picture turned black with ink. The smile was gone. That brought a happy little curve on his mouth and an order to his jerky breaths.

For the first time in the day, he felt at peace.

17
HAIRPIN BEND
Archana

TEN YEARS AGO...

They caught me in no time.

I ran the fastest I could, my lungs gasping for air, the threat to my life urging me to run faster, my senses becoming the most alert, but nothing worked. When one of the thugs caught me and pushed me into a car, my bones screamed in agony. I thought I was powerful and that I could get in and out of anything using my brains. That moment, when my bones were being jammed against his knuckles and the door handle, it humbled all my pride.

The pain blurred my vision. I was a weakling. A pesky mouse in the hands of a human. I knew fighting back was useless. Despite that, at some point, I tried to land a few punches in the thug's gut. No use. All my punches bounced back like I had punched a rock. My knuckles hurt. He twisted my arm and pushed me inside the car.

I screamed at the top of my voice and was immediately shushed by filthy gags. They pushed one into my mouth and tied the other around it. I could barely breathe. Muffled screams and tears came out. Nothing else. They were taking me away. This was bad. I saw the make and model of the car when they shoved me in. A Tata Sumo—TN 3985. I kept repeating it in my head.

How would I let Deva know where I was? My head raced.

Deva wouldn't know how to track my GPS. He wouldn't be calm in circumstances like these. He would just not think. He would just react.

Being calm during times like this is extremely important. Even a small impulsive step would cost my life. A knot grew in the pit of my stomach. Was I going to die? No. There were a lot of things to do. I couldn't just die; not in the hands of these muttonheads. Not yet.

Two thugs sat on either side of me, leaving no space for me to keep my arms in position. Their varying body odours raging inside the cramped-up space was too much to handle.

I needed someone who would think. Someone who stayed calm in situations like these.

Nikitha.

If only I could let Nikitha know and ask her to somehow contact Deva. She would know what to do. She could help me.

I had my phone with me. Good. These idiots had forgotten to retrieve my phone. And they hadn't tied me. Yet. All I had to do was text an SOS message to her. She would do the needful. She knew every little detail about my association with Deva, and she had warned me not to do anything stupid. I wondered if she'd be angry. I looked outside the window.

"Tie something around her eyes," Gunasekaran said from the front seat. The thug on my right did as he was told. Only my nose was sticking out. I had lost almost all the senses. I had no idea what to do. My phone was inside my laptop bag, which was on my lap, and I was clutching it tight. In time, they would obviously take the bag from me and tie me to some tree or a concrete block or… I had to stop panicking. Overthinking stuff wasn't going to do any good.

I had to retrieve my mobile before they snatched the bag away from me. I ran my fingers around for the zipper, and the moment I caught it, I pulled it up slowly without making any noise. After the zipper was up a few inches, I reached my hand in, feeling slowly for the mobile. The heat from my laptop was a tad comforting. My breaths turned jerky as I felt the sleek metal of my mobile. I pulled it out gently, hid it in the shallow of my palm, brought it up against my chest and dropped it inside my kurti. It fell in and the underband of my bra held it in place. I had no idea if the thugs saw me doing this, as my eyes were tied shut. But considering there was no reaction from them, I assumed they hadn't. I heaved a tiny sigh.

The car twisted and turned. It had been more than an hour since I had been thrown inside the car. Where were they taking me? Each passing minute was painful and scary. I was parched because of the cloth inside my mouth. I pointed to my mouth again and again. One of the thugs untied my mouth, pulled out the cloth from inside and passed me the water bottle. I opened the lid and downed the contents.

There was absolute silence in the car apart from the sound of me drinking the water. Would they take pity on me? Because of the fact that I was gulping the water like a cow? I hoped they would. Hope is a cruel thing…more than grief, regret or anything else, but we don't realize it unless we have felt it deeply. I felt it today. I had read this in one of Harlan Coben novels. I teared up. Will I ever get to read another after today?

"No need to tie my mouth," I said. "I won't scream. I know it's of no use."

Silence. I bet they were looking for an approval from Gunasekaran.

"You're a smart kid," I heard his voice.

Another hour passed before the car started taking more turns. I was getting nauseous.

Hairpin bends.

Damn it, we were headed for the summit of a hill. Where no one would find me if they dumped my body. My heart stopped for a second. Why the hell did they tie my eyes? I had to send a text to Nikitha. My pulse raced in fear.

"Call him," I heard Gunasekaran speak. "Tell Vijay that we have arrived with the girl."

18
HOW TO SLANDER? LEARN FROM THE BEST

10 December 2016

Coimbatore District Collector's Office

Deva and a few other villagers—his trusted ones—decided to meet the Coimbatore District Collector to explain the situation in the village and hasten the snail-paced process of justice. They took the bus to Coimbatore. The media drama worked just fine to spread the news and make it viral, but viral doesn't bring justice.

They left the village early in the morning and went to the collector's office at around eight; much before the collector had stepped in. They were made to wait outside the building. The group went to sit down under the shade of an old banyan tree inside the office premises.

Hours passed, but no one came. At around noon, the collector's white Ford swooshed in. The group, led by Deva, sprinted their way to the car and were held back immediately by the guards with harsh words.

"Move back you sickos!" said one.

"Silly villagers!"

Deva controlled his urge to punch them dead. He went back and sat under the tree. Another two hours passed by.

"Anna, I'm hungry," said a man from the group.

"Yes anna, we all are."

"We can't eat, I'm sorry," Deva said and patted him. "What if they call us while we are out eating? It's risky."

"You're right, anna," the man said and went back to waiting patiently.

Three more hours passed by and the scorching heat had dried up their throats. A stout peon wearing a pair of funny pants walked towards them with a sullen, disgusted expression on his face. He wore his loose pants so low that it revealed his entire pot belly and some more.

"You can go in now," funny-pants said. The entire group got up.

"Not all of you, you smelly lot. Just one," he said again and Deva clenched his fist so tight that the veins seemed to be popping out.

"Apologisz to my people right now or your face will be smashed to a pulp," Deva said.

Funny-pants laughed. "Or what?"

"Do not push me," he said calmly. The kind of calm that would invoke the darkest fears in you in a jiffy. That was how it was with Deva. "I'm here for my people. If you push me, you will be sorry."

This time, the spider veins on his neck broke out.

Two other peons came running towards him. "Back off, Chandran!" one said. "You don't know about him. He is Deva. He's all over the TV, didn't you see? If he smashes you, you're done for."

Funny-pants shrugged. "Whatever," he said, but clearly took a step back. "You go in and speak."

Deva towered over the man and passed him slowly with a piercing glare, as if he was staring right into his soul. Funny-pants held his breath and took three-four steps back.

When Deva entered the collector's office, he felt the stinging, cold air from the AC instantly drying up his sweat. Perks of power, he thought. If only his people who worked day and night had this sort of luxury for a day. What could he do to get them that?

He shook off the thoughts, folded his hands and stood in front of the big chair, his head bowed. In front of him sat a man in his early thirties, wearing a crisp blue oxford shirt and a brown blazer, his feet up on the table. The rose-gold metallic board had his name inscribed in bold letters—so bold and in black, as if the board was yelling his name out.

Thiru. KESHAVA KUMAR, I.A.S
DISTRICT COLLECTOR, COIMBATORE

"Sir, I'm from Achipatti," Deva started. "Recently, there was a bl-"

"Wait," the collector said, adjusted his blazer, took his recently released Apple mobile out, dialled a number and started talking. Just like that. Without any courtesy. The conversation involved some girl's marriage and how much they were spending for it and about somebody's son's graduation. All gossip. This was intentional, just to show Deva that whatever he was about to say was of the least importance to him.

The conversation lasted about half an hour, and he was made to stand the whole while. In spite of the AC, sweat beads popped on his body, which in turn were quick to evaporate, leaving him feeling a piercing chill in his body. Rage rose inside him. But this time he couldn't evoke fear in this man for his actions, the way he had done with Mr Funny Pants because of his power. He had to stay quiet for his people.

Deva closed his eyes, heaved a deep sigh, and waited patiently.

The conversation now revolved around someone's affair with a European girl who had apparently visited India on a tourist visa.

"Foreign chicks are always the best. Agree or not," Keshava Kumar said, his teeth glistening.

Deva clenched his fists and released it.

"The Indian ones have too many restrictions. As if they are so worth it!"

Clench. Release. Clench. Release.

"The cool worthy ones are the ones from abroad who have a thing for Indian men, unlike the useless brown ones here."

Clench. Release. Clench. Release.

The restrained anger revealed a tightness in Deva's face, which was blatantly visible. This irritated the respectable district collector.

"Okay, I'll call you back," he hung up, glaring at Deva. "What?"

"I'm Deva from Achipatti. I'm here to tell you about…"

"Cut the crap," he cut him short. "Do you think I don't know who you are and where you're from? And that useless issue in your stupid village?"

Silence. One whole minute passed. The two just glared at each other.

Clench. Release.

"Would you mind your words?" Deva said, forcing a smile, which came out deadly. "I have been patient for long, but this is not the way you can treat us. More than twenty people were blasted to pulp because of a stupid factory built by a stupid, evil person for a stupid purpose in my village. People who trusted this stupid factory were ready to take on risks for the stupid benefits that they offered. My people were blasted. The murder of twenty people is not stupid. If there is anything that's stupid here, it is seeing a person like you sitting in this respectable chair."

Keshava Kumar shifted in his chair. He slowly brought his feet down from the table. He leaned forward and placed his index finger on his chin.

"Look, Mr Deva," he said. Mister! Somehow, a tinge of humility can be evoked in jerks like him when an educated, strong person takes a hard stand against them. When their pride is challenged by someone as righteous as Deva, they have no other choice but to surrender with respect.

"Yes."

"Vijay is not a stupid person," Keshava said. "You and I both know. We can't touch him."

Deva laughed.

"You know what? Shame on you for saying that! I thought you were here to serve the nation. Had no idea you were serving goons. I regret coming here thinking that you would help us get justice. It would take me minutes to crush your so-called untouchable Vijay. But I thought I should get justice the *right* way for my people. Now I don't know what's right. Looks like I never will."

He walked towards the door, turned back and said, "I'm the one who is actually stupid," he sighed and his eyes grew moist, "to still believe in justice."

19
THE KISS OF DEATH

Archana

TEN YEARS AGO...
31 October 2006

I had no idea where I was but I was glad when they pushed me inside a room and bolted the door. I immediately threw the cloth that tied my eyes, reached into my bra, retrieved my phone, and texted Nikitha.

"I have been kidnapped. Looks like a hill. Track my phone. Inform Deva. He is already on the way to CBE north. I'm scared, Niki. Save me."

I put the phone back in my bra, only to realize that I was weeping when I texted the last line. The fear had gotten to me now. I looked around. The room was pitch dark. I stumbled to reach a wall, and I sat down, resting my back on it. Why were they holding me in a room? Why hadn't they killed me yet?

I heard a sigh. A literal human sigh!

From near me.

"What the ..." I jumped out of my skin and landed on my left.

"Hey," I heard a voice say. The lights came on, too bright, blinding me. I turned around to look at the face I had addressed as cute for so long. The face of the man Deva was trying to destroy. The face that, even now, looked sweet and harmless. My blood hummed in fear.

I was in his office. There was a big table with a metallic name plate with the name 'Vijay Kumar' on it.

"Happy to finally see you," he said, and even his voice seemed fragile, like a harmless high-schooler.

"Why am I here?" I asked him.

"Oh, you know why."

I stayed silent.

"Guess you texted your boyfriend," he said. "I hope he is on the way."

I shut my eyes as I felt my heart produce aching thuds.

"You were so stupid, weren't you?" he asked, still smiling. Not a tinge of anger on his face. How did he do that? The more he appeared sweeter, the more menacing he seemed. "You believed the video and went directly to him. I knew you'd do something like this."

"What do you want from us?" I asked, tears streaming down my face.

"You know what gave me happiness?" he asked. "It wasn't building this company, or growing rich, or creating this empire." He paused. I waited. "It was when that righteous son of a bitch threw tantrums at the construction site every day."

My blood hissed slowly as my eyes grew wide.

"Every day when he came beating his chest, accusing me, threatening me, I felt alive. I felt on top of the world as if I was doing the right thing. Seeing him helpless and insignificant made me feel grand. Do you understand what I'm saying? He made me feel grand."

"You're sick," I said after he waited for my reply. He laughed.

"But after a while, it stopped. The tantrums stopped. I felt lost. I knew someone was helping him stay calm. Someone was helping him think clearly. That was wrong. Him being muddled and confused and helpless was my strength. If he started thinking straight, I would lose. I shouldn't let him think straight."

I glared at him through my tears. Every word he uttered made me feel nauseous.

"Now, you're here. You're the reason I felt lost. You tell me. What should I do with you?"

With that, he came near me and punched me square in the chest. The mobile in my bra hit my sternum and jittered, the pieces slicing into my skin. My eyes widened in shock as the wind got knocked out of my lungs. Before I could react, he hit again.

Once. Twice. Thrice. The fourth punch landed on my face, cracking my nose.

I felt the first punch. Only the first, because the pain it caused blurred my senses, especially my vision. I felt my nose crack. My head hummed in pain as blood oozed from my chest and face and dripped to the ground. The second, third and the next few punches did not give me pain. Instead, they sent me into a state of shock. I fell backward. He didn't stop. He kept punching me until I saw black.

When I woke up, I felt a sharp, stinging, burning sensation on my neck and a dull, deeper ache in my chest. The pain was so intense that I screamed in agony at the top of my voice. I blinked away my involuntary tears to make my vision clear. I was no longer in his office. I saw tree tops, bright sunlight through the gaps in the leaves, scratches of clouds on the sky, and I smelt the intoxicating scent of mud around me. I also saw a face.

Vijay's.

He was standing over me, sprinkling water on my face and then slapping me hard. My vision blurred in pain and anger. I had been brought into the woods. Murdering and burying me here would be a piece of cake.

"You were in love with him, weren't you?" he asked, holding my hair. His voice was still calm. My slowed-down heart picked up pace. And the instant it did, the pain grew sharper everywhere on my body, and my vision grew blurrier. I blinked.

"Ever had sex with him?" he asked, gritting his teeth through his smile. "You're such a pretty thing, aren't you? But I think that piece of shit was righteous enough not to touch you." He used my hair to pull my head up and banged it back on the ground. I shrieked in shock and exhaled. I opened my eyes. The vision was clear now, though a new pain shot up inside my head.

I tried to say something. He leaned closer and put his ear near my mouth.

"L-loser," I said after a lot of difficulty. My lips barely moved.

He lifted his head up and glared. I gave a cold stare back, geared up all my strength, and spat at him. It landed on his chin. He wiped it and smiled.

"You're a virgin, aren't you? You sure seem like it." He spoke calmly. "It's a shame if it's going to waste. Such a beautiful thing like you," he said and brushed his lips against my lips. I turned away in disgust. Tears rolled down my cheeks as I shut my eyes. Terror spread through me. "You should lose your virginity before you go. Consider that a gift from me for your smartness." He spoke again with that sweet smile on his face.

He climbed on top of me and slowly unhooked my kurti, retrieving the jammed cell phone out from my bra. He threw it away and stripped me off. I couldn't move. He looked at me from head to toe and took his time in doing so.

"You're so damn beautiful," he said, his eyes twinkling. He said it with so much truth and passion in it that I wished I had not heard it. He ran his palms on my body. His gentle caress hurt more than the wounds on my body. It was so disgusting that I felt like melting into the ground under his touch.

"No," I said. I thought I yelled in anger, but it came out as a silent, firm no.

I slowly brought my right arm towards him to push him off, but he twisted it the other way. My eyes peeled open in pain and I heard a gentle crack. The pain went searing through my body like wildfire. I let out a guttural scream that echoed amongst the trees and stayed there. I saw Vijay's face through my tears. He smiled at me, calm and composed.

"Ricky and Ron!" he squealed.

The thugs who were sitting near me in the car appeared out of nowhere and held me down. The one holding down my right arm did not care that it was broken. He pushed it to the ground and rested his knee on it. I screamed and cried and cursed. I couldn't handle the pain. I wondered how my heart didn't give away. Guess I was stronger than I thought. I bit my lip so hard that blood spurted out from it. One guy got on top of me and the other held me down.

I didn't feel anything else after that. Even though I did, I couldn't fight. My limbs were frozen. I felt numb, but the tears did not stop. I concentrated on everything other than the pain he was causing me. I concentrated on the treetops, the musty smell of moist mud, the bug that crawled near my face because of the smell of my blood, a flock of birds that happily flew by. I thought of Deva. His anger, his beard, his childlike excitement. I was going to miss everything. I was going to die. I did not wish to die. But the piercing pain tearing through my flesh from underneath made me think differently. I immediately wished I was dead, right there, right then.

They took turns to rip the life out of me and I didn't care. I had lost my body, and I didn't care. Nothing mattered. My life, my dreams, my values, my love. Nothing mattered as I lay on the ground like a piece of log, naked and vulnerable, yet ready to take on anything. Gladly, I didn't feel anything else after that. I think I did, but nothing mattered anymore. I let them do everything. The fight in me had died a painful death.

After what seemed like a lifetime, Vijay got up, panting, his face happy. The two other guys pulled their pants up and left the woods after nodding at their boss. Vijay nodded back and beckoned to someone behind me.

"Dispose her," Vijay said. "Carefully. Don't want police dogs snooping around. Take her inside and bury her. And if you want, you can also enjoy a piece of her before she dies." He looked at my naked body. "Damn, ain't she pretty? God, I haven't seen anything like her. Shame she sided with Deva," he wore his shirt back on and buttoned it as he spoke. "If she was on my side, I would have married her right now. Just look at that face and body, blood and dirt aside… God! Shame this mine of gold is now going to the mud. Shame!"

With that, I heard footsteps fading away. I wondered who Vijay was talking to, wondered who was going to eat me alive next.

With so much pain, I tried to turn my head around. One man walked towards me.

He was really big—bigger than the two thugs. I blinked to get a clearer look at his face. When I did, my heart stopped. I moved my eyes away from his face, and I saw it. An ice-cold hand reached for my hand, held it and squeezed it.

There was a snake tattoo on the arm.

He was the executor. I was right about him.

He came towards me and knelt beside me. His face was normal and mundane in a way that you would definitely overlook it if you passed him by in a crowd. If it hadn't been for his giant body, this man would have been invisible. Strange how the mind worked during a time like this.

I saw something strange on his mundane face. Something palpable but surprising. There were streaks of water on his face. He had been crying. I did not understand, but seeing the tears, I couldn't help. I started weeping too, but no sound came out. I gazed down. He had been clenching his fist tight and thumping on the bare ground with anger.

"A-Anna," I called out to him, extending my hand. "Don't. P-please."

He broke down on the ground and wept. I was shocked. It was strange to see a man as giant as him cry like a child. He was a good man. I cried along with him. When he looked at me again, I lifted my left hand and pointed to my naked body and broken hand and wept. He turned away, his eyes shut.

"Anna, save me," I said, though I knew I was going to die. My insides were jammed and my head was badly concussed. He immediately came closer to me, removed his shirt, and put it on top of me. He tried to wrap me in it, but my body was frozen in pain. He wept more as I winced in pain as he tried to put the cloth on me. He then wiped his tears and came close to me and said 'sorry'. His voice sounded feminine. I thought he was sorry because he was also going to rape me, in spite of the emotional breakdown he had had. But I was wrong. He gently wrapped me in his huge shirt and carried me up from the ground, making sure he did not hurt any injured part. The moment he lifted me, my jammed insides screamed in agony. But I stayed silent. I did not want them coming back.

"I'll save you," he said. "I'll save you." He cried and walked fast, as I held on to his thick arm with the snake tattoo. "I'll save you." His teardrops fell on my forehead, and I just couldn't stop crying. I held on to him tight. His big, stone-like bare body and his weeping heart were comforting. But sadly, I was zoning out. Everything twirled in front of my eyes.

"Oh shit," he said as he removed one arm of his from under my head and shook it. "Your head. It's bleeding." He touched the back of my head and showed his palm to me as he cried and walked fast. It was crimson. Maybe that's why I was having trouble seeing. My vision got blurry instantly. I was going to die.

"D-Deva will come," I said. "T-take me to him."

"I'm taking you to a hospital. We have got to hide."

"No use," I said. "I can't be saved. I'm going to die. Just take me to him."

I thought of my mom and dad. Tears escaped my eyes effortlessly and ran down my cheek. How would they react to the news? They were fragile. Deva. My mom. Dad. My dreams. Law. Vijay. The snake tattoo. The bug that crawled towards my blood—everything flashed in front of my eyes and circled around. I was passing out. This was bad.

"D-Deva," I said. Whenever I spoke, he brought his head closer to my face and I could smell pine from his hair. I distinctly noticed that. I also distinctly felt a sound that was following us.

Footsteps.

As if someone was running towards us. Was it Vijay? Did he know I was trying to be saved? My vision became clearer as my heart beat faster. The footsteps were fast.

Oh no.

I tried to stay awake, but something knocked him over and together we fell down on the ground. Even while falling, he made sure I landed on his body. The executor, I called him, but here he was, executing his will to save my life. Someone thwacked him from behind and I watched him getting punched, but I could not see the one punching.

"What the fuck did you do to her?" I heard a voice.

The voice I knew too well. I longed to get near the source of that voice. My heart ached as I tried to open my eyes. I saw him punching the tattoo-man again and again in the face. The executor did not try to stop the punches or explain. He just accepted them and laid on the ground. I wondered why. Probably because he felt he deserved it for letting me get raped.

"Deva!" I called out, trying to beckon him towards me. He let out a manly groan of pain, landed a hard punch on the tattoo-man's face and ran towards me and held me in his arms. I blinked to see his face clearly. He was crying so badly and slapping his forehead.

"Why did you go? Why?" He kept beating his chest and forehead and crying so much.

"Deva," I said. "H-He was trying to save me. H-He isn't bad." I tried to point to the tattoo man.

Deva's face changed. He threw a glance at the fallen, bleeding man and back at me. His eyes moved down on my body. The shirt apparently must have shifted, because I saw his eyes widen. He let out a guttural moan. I wept, and he hugged me.

"It's okay," he said, hugging me tight. "I'm going to save you, alright? I'm going to save you."

He gazed below, probably between my legs. I don't know what he saw, but he screamed aloud. Probably blood or scratches or bite marks or torn flesh or blood—I didn't know. Whatever it was, it made him grit his teeth and punch himself in his chest. He ran his hand so gently on the marks between my legs and I winced in pain.

"Those bastards." He groaned and immediately covered it up with the shirt. I held his hand to stop him from beating himself.

"Archana," he cried, hugging me tight. His arm was smeared with the blood from my head. He looked at it and cried hard again, embracing me.

"D-Deva," I said, pushing him away. "L-look at me," I said. He did, his face smeared with my blood, his tears running through that.

"Tell me Archana."

"I-I love you."

He paused for a second and started weeping even harder than before, caressing my cheek.

"Look," I said. "I'm going to die. You can't save me." I tried hard to speak. "I can explain why, but I can't t-talk."

He wept and beat his chest. By the time the shirtless tattoo-man came and sat near my feet and held them, tears fresh on his face. Deva looked at him and hung his head low.

"I want you to do something for me," I spoke.

"Tell me, Archana. I won't let you die. I won't. I can't." He began to hug me, putting my head in the hollow of his chest.

"Don't waste time." I pushed him away.

"Tell me. What should I do?"

I swallowed hard. My throat was parched. Seeing me swallow,

he rubbed my throat gently with tears in his eyes. This was the most beautiful touch ever in the entire day. I just wished it lasted longer.

"I want you to," I said and paused, "finish that kiss."

He stopped crying for a second.

"Please?" I said. That tattoo-man gave my feet an assuring squeeze, as if apologizing to me, got up and moved away.

"Please, Deva," I said. "I want to feel it. Do not send me away with their touch on my body. I want yours. I want you to leave your mark on my body before I leave."

"Don't say that." He started crying again. This time, his sobs were too hard and pain-stricken. I cried too as I held his palm tight. He brought his face close to mine, rubbed my hair off it and kissed my forehead, lingering for a few seconds as he sobbed. He smelled like himself—his raw scent—and I inhaled it again and again. I put my hand on his face, caressing his beard. I had wanted to do that for so long. But would this stubborn man have let me? No way. Now, he couldn't say no. In fact, he put his palm on mine, pulled it towards his lips and kissed it, while crying.

"F-Fraud," I said. He let out a sad smile and caressed my head. He looked darn handsome in spite of the smeared blood and the unending tears. That one smile undid the pain for me. I put my fingers on my lips, urging him to kiss it. He smiled again through his tears and heaved a sigh. He then put his fingers on my lips, looked at it with tears, caressed it, or wiped off the blood, I had no idea. But it was so magical. He brought his face close to mine, and I closed my eyes.

I felt his lips brush against mine gently. My dying heart started beating fast again. I hungrily puckered my mouth, opening it a little. He took it in wholly, sucking on my lower lip so gently. I had no idea how a rugged man like him could kiss so gently, like a feather. My girly instincts were triggered, but the more it did, it hurt me physically. He kissed so gently, without any force. Maybe he didn't want to hurt me more. I put my right arm on the back of his head and pulled him in hungrily for a proper kiss.

I felt my pain fade away slowly. The torn flesh between my legs, my cracked sternum, my broken left arm, my cracked nose; nothing mattered anymore, nothing bothered me anymore, because all my concentration was on my lips that were being magically treated by the love of my life. I felt at peace. When he moved away, his eyes were hazy and teary.

My head started twirling again, and my breaths turned shallow. I pointed to my neck. I had imagined him kissing my neck a thousand times. I had no idea why. It's just a girl thing. Maybe because that's one of the few places on a female body, which, when touched or kissed, makes us feel vulnerable, yet increases our trust threefold. They are extremely contradicting emotions, both invoked at ease, when done right.

He immediately reached for my neck and kissed me there, lingering the way he did on my forehead. I closed my eyes and exhaled the air from my lungs. His beard tickled me a bit, and I loved it. After a few seconds of kissing, he sobbed and buried his face in my neck like a kid. I cried too, caressing the back of his head, comforting him. I squeezed his palm.

I experienced the magical feeling spread throughout my body and heal me. I had no more thoughts. My vision blurred again, and the feeling of his kiss was fading too.

No. No. No.

I tried to stay awake. I tried to stay alive. But the more I tried, the more everything faded into oblivion. I could see Deva's face again, near mine, but not clearly. Everything blacked out. I was happy I was being held and cherished by the only man I could ever love. I felt my grip on his palm loosen, and that was the most painful thing I had felt in the entire day. I heaved a sigh. Or maybe it was my last breath.

However, I just knew I felt at peace when the force of life eased its way out of me.

20
FACE TO FACE

10 December 2016

Deva bought food for his companions on the way back from the collector's office. He requested them to eat heartily and apologized for being unable to feed them when they were hungry. They refused to eat.

"What do we do now, anna?" one asked.

"We wait. Patiently."

"I thought that was what we did today, and we were hoping they would definitely find a way."

"It doesn't come easy. We have to struggle. But please eat," he said, but they were stubborn. "For me."

Their faces instantly changed, and they agreed. Deva smiled.

"Aren't you joining us?" one of them asked.

"No. I'll stay here and try again with the collector. You finish off and go back to the village. I'll join you for dinner. Go safely," he said and pulled out his wallet to take out some cash. His face fell the moment he opened his wallet. His breaths turned erratic. He did not lay his eyes on the thing that had the tendency to rip his heart out and scatter the pieces all over the ground. But he knew it was there, behind those debit cards. As he held it, he could feel its presence. The passport-size photo he dared not lay his eyes on. The only thing that kept him going but also the only thing that made him paralysed at times.

His heart cried out, and he swallowed. He immediately pulled out the cash and handed it over to one of the guys.

"No, anna," he declined. "We have some money."

"Hold it now!" Deva pushed the money into his hands. "Don't you all drink it up. I'll whoop your asses," he smiled. "Keep it safe and use it when needed."

The guy hugged Deva. He hugged back tight. He wanted to break down and cry, but he played the bigger man and patted the boy's shoulder.

"Go safely now!" he bade farewell.

He knew it was of no use seeing the collector again. He had somewhere else to go. He dialled his friend in the city and borrowed his car for the day. He sat inside, pressed the accelerator and was headed to the hills.

To Kotagiri.

* * *

He wept as he drove; wept out loud after long as he hadn't had the time or space to do that. The yelling helped him calm down before meeting him. His nemesis. The chilly hill air, the green valleys, the breathtaking sound of the falls went unheard and un-felt as he drove through. He opened his wallet, sifted out all the card and bills, behind which was the passport-size photo of Archana. He pulled it out and looked at it as he pushed the brakes on the car. He wept again, this time his sobs quieter but the intensity so high that it gave him a pulsating headache. He turned the picture around. Her scribbling with an erasable gel pen, combining her name with his, made his heart ache. It had been ten years since it had happened.

Ten whole years.

Ten years since Archana was brutally raped and murdered.

Ten years since he lost his sleep. Ten years since he lost his appetite. Ten years since he lost his will to enjoy life. Ten years since his habits changed for the worse. Ten years of which not a night went by without hysterical crying, panic attacks and nightmares.

For ten years he had stayed quiet, waiting for the right time to nail him. It did not happen. Though he was angry, though he dedicated his entire life thinking of ways to kill Vijay, he hadn't done that yet. What was the point in claiming a life just because he took one? Death, according to Deva, was the biggest release. Why would he grant that privilege to someone sick like Vijay? Granting him a life in which he wished he were dead every day was what he wanted to give him.

He placed the picture carefully back into his wallet. Soon enough, he reached where he needed to be. He got out of his car and darted in. The minimalistic architecture of this place irritated him. Vijay never deserved to live like that. He deserved hell.

"Vijay!" Deva yelled the moment he was in the hall. "Come out, you bastard! Vijay, you spineless coward."

He yelled out a few curse words in Tamil. After seven whole minutes, Vijay came out in a pair of shorts and a towel in his hand and a smile on his face. Deva did not think twice. He ran up the stairs, reached Vijay and punched his face and chest. He did not stop. Vijay screamed in agony.

"Why did you kill her?" Deva asked. He must have asked Vijay this question a thousand times. But not once had he received an answer except a sarcastic, what-can-you-do-about-it smile that drove Deva crazy. Sometimes he hated himself for his righteous nature. Had he been just another man who would break the law and go to any extent for revenge, he would have murdered Vijay in the most gruesome way possible.

But every time he thought of it, something stopped him. Archana fell in love with him for his righteous nature, in spite of his impulsiveness. So did his dead wife. His son, though wouldn't mention it, was proud of his righteousness. And deep down, Deva knew it was his only strength. Anybody can go about and take revenge; but it took a real man to stay righteous and do it.

He probably was stupid to think so, and that thought haunted him. He knew he wouldn't change, he couldn't.

The punching did not stop. Blood spurted from Vijay's mouth. Deva kept launching punches at the face. He climbed on top of Vijay and sat on his torso, holding him down.

"Why did you kill her?" Deva asked and cried. He stopped punching. "Why?"

"Because I was afraid." Vijay spoke through his blood smeared teeth. He paused to spit the blood on the ground. "I was afraid she would help you. I was afraid I would fail."

"You could have killed me, why her?"

"Honestly? I liked her. She deserved to die."

Deva let out a deep groan and punched the face again and again. Vijay turned silent. He couldn't move. Deva hauled himself off the man, knelt down, and screamed. Vijay moaned in pain.

"Whatever you do," he said, letting out a painful moan. "You will lose."

"Is that so?" asked Deva, turning around to look at the fallen Vijay. "Is that what you think?"

"Yes. Your urge to do the right thing is the reason for your downfall," he spit out some more blood. "You can never win against me fair and square. I know you won't go for the crooked ways. If you did, you could have killed me right now. But you won't. See? That's where I win. I adore you, Deva. Your just nature is the reason why you're a loser. You're actually cute thinking that you could bring me down with your crap ideology. You're an idiot." Vijay grinned.

Deva laughed out loud in a ghoulish way. "Is that so?" he asked, still laughing.

The grin on Vijay's face was gone. He clearly did not like the smile on Deva's face. Something was wrong and he could feel it.

"I will tell you one word, Vijay. Just one word," Deva said, gazing deep into the man's eyes. "After that you tell me whether I can defeat you in a righteous way or not."

Vijay's pulse raced. He sat up straight, nursed his aching head, and took deep breaths. Deva moved towards him, pulled his chin closer, and looked him in the eye.

"What word?" Vijay asked.

"Christopher."

Vijay felt his entire body freeze in shock.

His heart stopped for a second and then raced. It was as though the name had sent an electric pulse through every vein in his body. His eyes widened and his face grimaced as if in deep pain.

Deva took in Vijay's reaction with a deep sense of relief. It was like meditation.

"You know what?" said Deva, his eyes shining. "I would take this face of yours to my deathbed."

With that, Deva left the poor, evil man to adjust to the shock while he turned away, climbed down the stairs, and walked out of the house.

21
TAKEN

10 December 2016
Achipatti Village

In Achipatti, the protest day had come to a peaceful end. Though Aadhi's eerie words at the end scared me a little, I felt better seeing uncle Deva. He was glad that the case had gone into good hands. I knew his visit to the district collector's office was bugging him, but we had expected nothing more. In spite of that, he seemed strangely happy that day, as if he had achieved something. I had no idea what was going on in his head. I didn't want to ask too, as long as he was happy.

We sat together on the terrace to eat *nila soru.* Moonlit dinner. Usually, our grandma would make one variety of rice—like lemon rice or puliyogare or sometimes even sambar rice, usually combined with some spicy potato fry and papads.

We wouldn't bring any plates. We would just take the drum of food and go upstairs. Our grandma would make enormous balls of the food, press them with her hand and pass it to us. Believe it or not, that food, in my opinion, is the tastiest food in the world. And somehow, our stomachs would be full soon and we would sleep like logs. Maybe it's because of the love that is infused into the food.

Usually, we had nila soru only when we were happy. But tonight, we wanted to have it for the sake of just being together. We wanted to stick together in doom. Our grandma had made bisibelebath, lemon rice, tamarind rice, three different chutneys, a large pan of potato fry, and a bowl of curd rice fried with mustard and curry leaves.

Comfort food.

We ate in silence as my grandmother passed around the balls. She had a tiny smile on her face—not of happiness, but of peace—for the fact that she was able to feed us well in such a time and that we were gobbling it up in hunger. She gave bigger balls of food to uncle Deva to show him that she loved him, was proud of him, and wanted him to heal. Through this ritual, we were all healing silently.

She added extra potato fries to my ball of rice. Extra tomato chutney in my dad's. Extra mint chutney in Aadhi's. And mostly gave curd rice to uncle Deva to cool his body. She knew our favourites and what we needed most.

As if on cue to ruin our peace, we heard footsteps scampering about on roads. Deva uncle rose with a start.

"Sit down now!" Grandma ordered and passed another ball of curd rice to him. Uncle denied.

"Something is wrong."

The next moment, the doorbell rang and Deva uncle sprinted downstairs. Aadhi and I followed him. It was Mani at the door, the guy in the lungi—one of uncle Deva's ardent disciples.

"Anna!" he cried, collapsing into uncle's hands. "They are arresting everyone. The police are arresting everyone."

"What?"

He held onto the puny man tight to stop him from shaking like a leaf.

"Our boys have all been arrested, anna, and they are coming for you."

"What?" Uncle Deva repeated, his eyes slowly turning red.

The next moment, Inspector Rajendran appeared with two stout, pot-bellied men on either of his sides. He had a despicable smile on his face.

"Mr Deva," Inspector Rajendran said. "You're under arrest. We are taking you to Pollachi station."

"Why?"

"For triggering the innocent villagers and trying to create a revolution for nothing."

"For nothing?" His eyes were crimson. "Really?"

"Yes. You triggered them for *nothing,*" he repeated, as if it didn't matter. "Come with me or things will get rough."

"This is not the way you talk, sir," Aadhi said, and uncle Deva signalled him to back off.

Uncle Deva guffawed. "Triggered them? That's a good joke."

"We have received a lot of complaints about you," Inspector Rajendran said, his face sullen.

"Complaints?" Uncle Deva was amused. "Real or fabricated? Oh, I'm sure they are all fake as a three rupee note."

"Excuse me?"

Deva uncle went closer, both the men towering against each other.

"I know you work for Vijay. I am not dumb," he whispered. "He got scared, did he? I scared the shit out of him!"

Uncle Deva said, and let out a ghoulish laughter. I didn't know what he meant, but it certainly had an effect on Rajendran. He glared hard at my uncle, clenching his fists.

"Stop it, Deva," a voice said from behind. It was my dad. He pulled uncle Deva away from the officer and the two exchanged words for a while. It looked as if my dad was explaining the situation and uncle Deva was listening with his head down. In a moment, he came back and held his hands out to the inspector.

"Arrest me," he said. The inspector was mildly taken aback but pretended not to show it. He obliged, though, and uncle Deva was cuffed right in front of my eyes.

We had no idea what to do.

"Be patient," my dad whispered to us. "Let him go."

Aadhi's eyes widened, and he nodded immediately.

"What?" I asked him.

"He is safer there," Aadhi said as we watched our only pillar of hope being escorted out by the police.

* * *

Four others were arrested along with uncle Deva, his secretive right hands—the primary executors of all his plans to help people. No one other than our family knew about them. We wondered how the police, or the force that's operating these khakis, even had an idea about them. At that moment, I realized I had been underestimating Vijay Kumar. uncle Deva's confusion amidst all the magnificent effort and Aadhi's agonizing fear in spite of his dad's heroism were all sane.

I swallowed hard as I saw my uncle being escorted out by the police. A cognitive punch landed in my gut. What if they do something to uncle Deva in the prison? It was a relief that he was just five kilometres away from the village, but I had heard of a lot of incidents where the police would go to any extent to get what they needed. Especially if there was a chance they were being heavily funded by biggies. Uncle Deva was rich too, but he wouldn't ever bribe these khakis.

Aadhi held my hand.

"They won't do anything," he said.

"How do you know?" I said, my voice cracking. Wind blew through the open door and it was then I felt the cold streaks on my face. I had been crying.

"Because they know they would face something money can't save them from. The wrath of people."

22
POLITICS = POLY-TICKS

We had an inside man at the police station. As I mentioned before, a lot of police officers admired Deva uncle to an extent that they would put their jobs at risk to help him. One such man was Sub-Inspector Syed. Newly recruited, young, spontaneous, fiery, proficient, and someone who respected his job more than his superiors. This had led him to be extremely liked by the topmost superiors and loathed by the immediate ones. Naturally, he wasn't allowed inside the interrogation room by Inspector Rajendran.

But we were getting updates from him on the proceedings. Loads and loads of talking and nothing more. Tons of long questions by various officers and one word or at times no reply from uncle Deva. It was a wave of relief for us. We knew they hadn't laid their hands on him. Aadhi was right. Money couldn't buy everything.

"Thank you, Syed anna," I said to him as he was washing up the plate at our house. We had just invited him over for lunch, and in the meantime, listened to his hour-long tale about the incidents at the station.

"Don't worry, Shravya. I won't let anything happen to Deva bhai," Syed said. He was a well-built man and was insanely fair. After his mother's death, he had vowed to give up the one thing that he craved for. And hence, he quit non-veg in spite of being a staunch Muslim. He had a younger sister who was spastic. She was his world, and he took care of her like a child. Uncle Deva played a major role in taking care of her medical expenses.

Achipatti had a mosque and a dargah, one big church and many temples. No other village in our surrounding had places of worship other than temples. But our village was different. For decades, we were used to visiting mosques during all sorts of sickness and the dargah for hauntings which were common in the countryside. Our villagers were one in spite of the religious scuffles in cities that were triggered and funded by anti-national organisations.

In Achipatti, we honoured everyone's religious practices and way of life. We respected humanity, love and peace more. Syed was the best example of this. I had always felt Syed was something of a reincarnated version of Dara Shikoh—Aurangazeb's elder brother, who focussed on leading and teaching the purest way of life.

Syed opened the gate to leave, and the creak reminded me of what happened to Dara Shikoh in the end. I just wished Syed didn't meet his end like Dara. My breath snagged, and I felt a dull ache in my gut. Bad thing to think about when Syed was leaving our house. I watched him walk away until his figure faded. And in that moment, a chill ran down my spine.

The media's attention on the blast case grew, and political leaders from all over Tamil Nadu started visiting Achipatti with money worth peanuts to throw at the victims, forcefully accumulated crocodile tears ever ready to flow out in public, and an army of media to capture the best angles of those shots.

Our sorrow was just another platform for them to perform their political stunt. And the villagers, though they knew about it, couldn't help but welcome them, hoping that there would be a silver needle in the dirty haystack—a good politician that would help them and imprison Vijay.

Our family knew better. Every politician who wanted to enter our village had to pass by us first to get the approval of our people. Though they loathed us, they had no choice. Starting with the village ward councillor to the Minister for Rural Development of Tamil Nadu, Mr Ponnudurai, and the Health Minister Mr Kalingaraj, visited Achipatti.

Mr Kalingaraj was known for being the most educated state minister. When he was elected, people celebrated, saying that finally there was someone educated who had the seat. I agree education is important for a politician. However, there is no guarantee that education will make you a good person. Wonder how the people always blamed the educated people for all the havoc in the world and considered the uneducated as innocent, but still wanted an educated person to rule them. If there was something I learnt about society, it was just that it's a toxic, sparkling peak of hypocrisy and lies. And it sets expectations that are *not* to be met.

A person is expected to be good, study well, marry within the caste, should not fall for petty things like love, and be an ideal individual, which mainly includes killing his personal desires. And if someone meets these expectations, the society will declare that there is something else that *has* to be wrong with him, probably out of jealousy or with the sole intention of spewing venom.

The politicians greeted us with so much respect and shared their overflowing sympathy for the people. For a moment, it all felt real until they paid an amount to each of the victim's family—a petty amount of one lakh.

"Sir, we don't need the money," Aadhi said to Kalingaraj. "We need justice."

Mr Kalingaraj let out his practiced laugh and put his arm around Aadhi. "Of course, of course, thambi. But first, let us do what's needed."

"What's needed," Aadhi said and paused to clench his teeth, "is justice, Sir," He said the word 'justice' with so much grit that the villagers who heard it started roaring to express their support. Kalingaraj responded with a stare. The smile had faded and in place of it was an empty face and hollow eyes that felt like tiny darts to the soul. Aadhi glared back, not moving a hair.

"Yes. Yes," he said and turned to the people. The empty eyes came back to life. The crowd fell silent, their ears cocked. "The conspirator will be given the highest order of punishment," he said. "My people are dead. Mine! Do you think I will let that go? They trusted this factory and left farming to work here and they were murdered. If I let this matter go to the bin, what kind of human am I, let alone a politician? I'm not asking you to trust ıne. But I'm just begging for a chance to prove to you that I still love my people. I'm a politician, yes. But it is not fair that I'm presumed to be a dishonest human being because of other scumbags in the industry. I only hoped to help as many people as possible, and the only path is politics. Do you think it's my mistake?"

Wow.

I swallowed an invisible lump in my throat as I, an average school girl, sympathized with the state minister. I wondered how they did that!

The entire village listened keenly; their jaws slightly open. Only one person heaved a tremendous sigh of boredom. Aadhi. I shushed him as the minister's empty eyes chanced a glance at him, sending a shiver down my back.

"I know some of you still don't believe me. But can you do the honour of giving me little time? I will do what is needed."

The people, before they knew, nodded in sync. Applause rose a little. The empty eyes turned to Aadhi, probably expecting the same and Aadhi responded with an uninterested set of claps, just to show that he would be ready to flatter the man as long as he helped the villagers. Kalingaraj smiled. I wondered why Aadhi's assent seemed so important to them.

They knew uncle Deva's blood was as hot as his, or even hotter. That was the reason for the intimidation and the yearning for his approval and appreciation.

"But for now," he raised his hand to quieten the crowd while he secretly wished they didn't. "I really want you to take the money. Think of it as my offering to God. I'm your devotee. I always have been. And I'm offering you this with all my heart." He took a long pause as he let the wave of approval set in the crowd. Then he went for the killer punch. "God never says no, does He?"

Done and dusted.

Money received. Hugs exchanged. Tears wiped. Food served. And at the end of the day, the minister's pure white shirt became soiled with the sweat and tears and dirt of the lamenting villagers, and he didn't seem to mind.

"Maybe he is a good man," I said. "I have read about him. No scams, nothing. Very well educated. His speeches give goosebumps."

"Ah, he's just a good talker. I can give you that," Aadhi said, downing the umpteenth cup of buttermilk. Curry leaves and mustard floated on top.

"But not a good man?"

"Nope."

"How can you be so sure?"

"Because he is a politician." He licked the edge of the plastic cup to make sure not a drop went to waste.

"That's unfair!" I said, pulling away the empty cup from his hand, crushing it and throwing it away.

"What? I don't like wasting food!"

"Not that. You are judging Kalingaraj just because he is a politician. He just cleared things up in his speech. One shouldn't judge him."

"Like I said, he's a good talker." He reached for the next cup of buttermilk, but I stopped him.

"I don't believe you. You're so untrusting. Deva uncle isn't like you."

"Yeah, he's the opposite. He trusts everyone. That's why I'm like this," Aadhi chortled.

I glared without saying a word.

"Fine. I'm with you," he gave in. "Kalingaraj *might* be a good man. Let's give him a chance. Let's see if this politician stands by his word for once."

* * *

Two days passed. We stayed silent; our bodies paralysed. Constable Syed sat on the thinnai near Aadhi and my dad, and in front of them were the villagers, on the verge of tears. Some sat with a blank countenance, some with their faces buried, and others with one hand on their puny chests.

"I just got to know," Syed said silently, hoping the tone of his voice would calm his people. "I'm shocked just like you."

We had come to know from Syed that Kalingaraj is none other than Vijay Kumar's father-in-law's own brother. This was never revealed to the media. Kalingaraj was unmarried, and hence, nobody cared to know about his family. If he had had a dumb wife who had a face or some antics for the camera, probably people would have cared. The kith and kin of politicians are interesting to the people only if they are controversial. The bottom line was that nobody knew about his family.

Syed had smelt something fishy while witnessing yesterday's talk-of-the-town speech of the minister and had started digging. None of the official records had the details of his family. But hail Google! It tattles affairs, money trails and scams in a jiffy if used properly.

There was one picture of him hugging Vijay Kumar in a private family gathering, clicked by a small-time magazine reporter, who had sneaked his way in somehow. The pictures were released for entertainment in his popularly unread magazine called '*Maasa Malar*' to show the 'unseen face' of the health minister. Him enjoying and having fun and smiling—him being a human--had become an 'unseen face'.

Lousy vultures! Anyway, this vulture had helped Syed.

Two pictures of Kalingaraj hugging and playfully punching another older man whose striking features were similar to the politician—empty eyes, well-defined jawline, killer smile. Maybe Vijay's dad? Nope. He passed away when Vijay was very young. Kalingaraj's brother sure, but related to Vijay. How?

The next few pictures answered Syed's queries

A woman with facial features shockingly similar to Vijay's wife—a fair, pimpled face, eyes uncannily large, and wide apart and unusually small lips—joined the duo, her hand on the old man's stomach, as if stopping the blows. Family love.

Busted.

The woman was Vijay's mother-in-law and obviously the old man's wife. The old man was Kalingaraj's elder brother or probably the brother who aged soon due to trauma.

Whatever it was, Syed was sure that Kalingaraj was connected to Vijay. He held out the printouts of the pictures to the villagers, rubbing salt into their wounds intentionally, maybe because he thought they deserved it for trusting someone so soon, falling for their words.

Aadhi gave a 'I-told-you-so' glance to me and I looked away.

"That cow!" a villager said. "I had tears when he said he would throw the conspirator behind bars."

"His choice of words! Don't judge me because I'm a politician. I'm a human, too. Human, my foot!" another said.

"We are doomed! What do we do?"

"Shame we took his cursed money. What I would do to throw it back on his face!"

Aadhi's countenance turned stiff. "You know what?" he said. "Let's do that. Let's give back the money without telling them why. Let the minister just know that we were unhappy with him for some reason. Let's not rat out the fact that we know he is connected to Vijay."

"Why not?" I asked. "He should know we found out. He should know that Achipatti people are smart and not suckers for money."

"Yeah, she's right!" someone said from the crowd.

"Shravya's right. I agree," another said.

"Yeah, Kalingaraj should know!"

I threw a haughty look in Aadhi's direction.

"Well..." Aadhi held out his hand and the villagers turned quiet instantly, the way they did with uncle Deva. "If we say that, we would have to tell how. And Syed would be in danger."

"I don't mind," Syed said.

"Sorry, anna," Aadhi said. "I can't let that happen."

The villagers murmured. "Aadhi is right," they said and I rolled my eyes.

"We will just return the money. That's punishment enough," someone said.

"Punishment?" one guffawed. "He doesn't give a rat's ass about us!"

"Guys...guys!" Aadhi said. "Enough. Leave it to me," he looked away from them. "I'll handle it."

The next day, the media was summoned, who came to us at lightning speed. Achipatti's story was in high demand. Aadhi had demanded a live session with the famous local news channel Surya TV. They agreed immediately and even sent their best reporter to interview Aadhi for the Live.

Facing the reporter, Aadhi spoke.

"We have decided to give back the compensation that the honourable Health Minister, Mr Kalingaraj, gave to us. This is to let him know that we venerate justice and nothing else. Sir, we don't need your money to help us get by every day. We have got it, and even if we don't, that's fine. We don't mind dying of hunger rather than eating food from the money scraped out of our loved ones' carcasses. But again, we respect that you stepped forward, and we don't mind taking the compensation, too, but only when our basic demands are heeded to. I'm not sure if you actually care about us taking the money or not. But we want you to know that your job with our village hasn't ended by throwing some pennies at us. So, here's the deal, respectable minister. If what you said yesterday in Achipatti is true, we would like you to prove it."

He paused and then continued. "One, we need some kind of update in this case. There has been no significant progress. We need the owner to be interrogated at least once. And two," Aadhi paused. The reporter's eyes were intent, as if aching for his next word, "I need my father to be released," he said. "Keeping him locked up and leaving us in the dark won't work. We need him back. Only here, the criminals are let go and the only man who is fighting for justice is imprisoned. If petty things like money, your political position or reputation," Aadhi paused, "or if your love, connections, family or your protective instincts stop you from giving us justice, then this is what we stand by."

Aadhi pointed to a space behind him. The camera panned immediately.

All the cheques worth lakhs were arranged in a heap as the villagers surrounded it. One man held a can of kerosene. The camera panned back to Aadhi again.

"Please don't think we are dumb, sir. We aren't dogs to wag our tails for money. We already lead a richer, riper life than many in this fertile land. But when our lives are hindered, we rebel. If we don't get an update soon about the two things I have asked for, we don't mind burning the money. It is not to disrespect you, sir. But it's just to show that we need justice! Us burning lakhs of money might be of the least concern to you. But imagine what it does to your reputation. So, are you going to protect your loved ones or bring us justice?"

My jaw went slack. He did not just say that!

The reporter frowned at the last sentence. "I didn't quite catch that, Aadhi," she said. Aadhi stayed silent, his eyes glued to the camera, as if he was staring at the minister himself.

"Protect your loved ones or bring justice? Seems contradictory, doesn't it? Are you trying to say that the villagers aren't his loved ones?" she pointed the mic at him.

Aadhi laughed. "I'm sure the minister would understand. Thanks for the Live."

As soon as he moved away from the camera, I caught him. "You did not just say that on camera!"

"Say what?" he reached for the plastic cup of buttermilk.

"Twice you indirectly mentioned his connection with the owner. One when you mentioned love and protective instincts, and hell, the last line! Do you think the reporter is dumb? She would have known by now."

"And so would the people."

I glared at him as he relished a curry leaf.

"You're threatening a state minister. This doesn't look good."

"I'll do what it takes," he said and reached for another cup.

* * *

23
TURBOCHARGED TACTICS

24 December 2016

Two weeks passed by quietly. We once visited uncle Deva at the police station. He had not been put in prison. He was just being held for the entire day, interrogated, and was given a room with a cot at night. He was fed well and was well taken care of, probably to keep the people from creating a ruckus. Then why were they holding him? Probably to show us that no matter who shouts on the streets, they are the boss.

Uncle Deva seemed forlorn, mostly because he missed us.

"Don't worry about me," uncle Deva said, as I was hugging him and soiling his T-shirt with tears while Aadhi held his hand tight. His familiar scent felt like a comfort, and I inhaled again and again.

"Come back," I said.

"I will. They are holding me for some reason. Let them. I'm sure they won't do anything because of my people outside. This is just pure drama."

We didn't say anything.

"I saw your Live yesterday," he said, looking at Aadhi. "Bold. Too good!"

Aadhi relished the praise, his chest inflated. His childlike glee was obvious and his urge to still get an approval from his father was cute. He hugged Deva uncle, burying his face in his shoulder.

That hug involving the three of us lasted for one whole minute or more. Deva uncle didn't let us go. His familiar fragrance quietened our souls.

It felt like home.

After we came back home, we didn't have much to do. I took a good, long nap—something I hadn't done for days together. Maybe the hug from uncle Deva had calmed my chaotic mind. When I woke up, I realized I had slept for twelve hours straight, drooling all over my pillows.

I had to go back home to Coimbatore and make up for my lost school days, but I didn't want to leave Aadhi alone. However, my dad took me back to the city, where I led a normal life—went to school, came back home, studied and went about my daily chores—a life with no excitement, my heart fully affixed on Achipatti, looking for updates.

Aadhi's Live went viral, and he became a small-time hero. Even YouTubers from other states visited Achipatti to cover the issue and interview Aadhi. Things were fine until I sat down in front of the TV, with a bowl of jackfruit on my lap. The news was on.

One headline caught my attention, and I stopped chewing. My head felt dizzy and my lips unknowingly curved into a ghoulish smile, or a laugh came out, I couldn't tell. The breaking news flash came on the screen yet again.

'Veera Explosives blast case has been transferred from the Coimbatore Police to the CBI. Owner Vijay Kumar taken in for interrogation.'

What!!!

I literally jumped. CBI meant good news. No space for tomfoolery or buying officers with money. Other breaking news pieces followed. I waited for the decked-up woman in the pretentious saree to speak about the first news in detail. There she came.

"On December first, there was a blast at the Veera Explosives factory in Achipatti due to some error. Over fifteen people were killed in the blast," she spoke with zero expression or empathy on her face.

Fifteen? What the fuck?

As far as we knew, over twenty-five families were mourning. Why reduce the number?

"Protests broke out in the village against the owner of the factory, Mr Vijay Kumar, who heads a successful business conglomerate with a number of reputed explosives factories under his name. The Tamil Nadu government is a regular purchaser of his products."

I felt anger surging through me. Had Vijay bought this channel too? Why the heck were they glorifying him?

Ass-kissing scoundrels, I thought.

She went on. "The people demanded to shut down the factory and to arrest him. When honourable Health Minister Kalingaraj went to Achipatti village to offer compensation, the people turned it down, heeding to a young man named Aadhi, the only son of Deva, whose monologue went viral." Her eyes moved from right to left as she read from the prompter.

On the side of the screen, they were playing Aadhi's Live, his voice muted.

That moment, my pulse raced. Why would they repeatedly show Aadhi's face on TV? Till then I thought it was free publicity for the issue, but at that moment, I felt like he was in some danger.

"He had put up two demands straight to the health minister, challenging him to fulfil them. And it looks like the minister has done that! The Achipatti blast case has been transferred to the CBI due to the continual mystery and uncertainty that surrounds the case, and also the undying seriousness."

Over twenty-five people were blown to a pulp, bitch! Continual mystery, is it?

A visual of Vijay being escorted by the police was shown on the screen. His twisted, yet handsome, face seemed very forlorn. It was a happy sight.

Good. Good. Good. I thought as I began to get reckless.

I grabbed my phone to call dad.

His number was busy. Apparently, he had already got a call from the village. I scrolled up to find Aadhi's name. But the screen lit up with his name. I got an incoming call from him.

"Aadhi!" I squealed. "Did you watch the n..."

"Kalingaraj is back in the village," he cut me short. "Inform Appa."

It didn't take long for us to go to the village. Me and my dad. He kept my mother out of this. He wished to keep everyone out of this, but I was not in on the being kept out idea. He didn't have the time to pursue a pointless argument with me when he knew I would win. We were happy there was significant progress in the case, but we had no idea why the minister was back. Was Aadhi in trouble?

"What happened?" Dad asked uncle Rudran, as his house was crowded with the villagers. "Why is he back?"

"No idea. The press, the police, they are all here. Big press, anna! National ones. Don't know what they are going to do."

"Are they going to do something to Aadhi?" Dad voiced my thoughts and my stomach did a somersault.

"No way! It's because of Aadhi that the case went viral. People are talking about it. I feel this is something else. He has asked the people to gather at the factory. Let's go!"

Aadhi was nowhere to be found and my head felt a little dizzy.

"Without Deva everything is a mess," dad said. Everything seemed wrong. We took Rudran uncle's car to go to the factory from his house. As we passed by the eerie lane, I shut my eyes. Everyone in the car, who had tons of things to discuss, uncannily quietened down. The lane to the factory seemed even creepier after the death of the villagers.

I hadn't opened my eyes, but I knew exactly when we had crossed the dark lane. I heaved a deep sigh. The chattering continued. I saw what uncle Rudran was talking about. People from the surrounding villages had assembled there. Press vans' engines purred with excited reporters sprinting out of them, mouthing hurried instructions to cameramen. A number of white cars were visible in the front.

We got down and pushed our way to the cars. A swarm of people joined hands and protected Kalingaraj as he got out and reached his way to the small stage that Deva uncle's men had built for him. He had a big smile on his face. Though he expected the people to cheer for him, he did not let the stark silence of the people affect him even a bit. Maybe it did, but his face did the honour of not letting it show.

"I'm sure you have all heard by now that the case has been transferred to the CBI. We are in good hands now." He said, trying not to sound too excited.

"We have access to the news, sir," said a young man from the crowd. Kalingaraj's eyes darted to the spot the man. He couldn't.

"Also, like Aadhi thambi mentioned, I have done the needful to get Vijay arrested. He would be juiced out by the CBI. Guess I do care about justice more than my *loved ones.*"

My stomach turned at the statement. I felt a knot as I saw the minister's empty eyes take a dive towards Aadhi and stay there. Aadhi did not move a muscle. He let it pass, his face calm as if to sarcastically ask if there was any other counter to his statement. Nothing.

The people just looked keenly at him as if to ask him, "All that's fine. But what is your business now in Achipatti?"

"I came here to do one last thing," he said. "I know you don't trust me. You do not trust anyone during this horrible time, and it is understandable. If I could bring back the innocent souls, I would go to any extent to do that. Not to prove that I'm trustworthy, but because I want you to know that this hurts me..." he paused as his smile faded. "The fact that your loved ones are gone hurts me. And I know I can't bring them back, no matter what I do. But there is someone I can bring back."

He pointed to his car, and immediately, his underling sprinted towards the door and pulled it open. The villagers craned their neck to look.

Out came a man in a flimsy T-shirt, with a fit physique and a remarkable scar on his temple. My heart screamed.

Uncle Deva.

I felt paralysed with happiness. The villagers hailed him and ran towards the car, ignoring the minister and his unsavoury attempt at winning their hearts back. They hugged him tight and he couldn't hold back his tears. He wept like a child on his people's shoulders and they wept more, holding him so tight that I felt his bones might give way any moment. I touched my face and realized I had been crying. This had been happening to me quite often these days. In spite of the surge of emotions, his eyes immediately started looking for me and Aadhi and we raised our hands. He waved at us. We waved back and signalled him to enjoy the attention.

He deserved it, the hero that he was!

Uncle Deva's forlorn face turned the opposite as the villagers lifted him high and swirled him around like a puppy.

"Deva anna!" yelled a voice. "Hail!"

The villagers joined him and shouted praises in Tamil as Kalingaraj stood silently on the stage, twirling the mic between his fingers. Probably this was the first time he had been ignored so blatantly in his entire life.

I would be lying if I said it didn't give me a good feeling. My eyes were fixed on the minister and I took pleasure in seeing him ignored. Though he was doing the right thing, something didn't fit.

The villagers carried uncle Deva towards the stage and dropped him near Kalingaraj. One man in a lungi respectfully took the mic from the minister's hand and handed it to uncle Deva.

Uncle Deva looked at the crowd and said just one line.

"I won't stop until we get justice."

I was sure that the roar I heard that day would stay with me forever.

24
CELEBRATIONS BEGIN

Needless to say, Deva uncle's return was celebrated like the return of a long-lost son. It was a subtle celebration considering the multiple deaths in the blast, but people still overcame their grief to cherish uncle Deva's presence because he was their only hope. They weren't celebrating uncle Deva. They were celebrating hope.

Though it was supposed to make us happy, it was deeply painful. Painful to see the smiles on the swollen faces of the victim's family members. Painful to see them hugging uncle Deva as if he were their dead son or husband or dad. When they were supposed to let the grief gnaw at the soul, they had *allowed* hope to heal them, and that was beautiful, yet so painful to watch.

We can help someone only if they let us. There is a high chance that the trauma and pain become a huge part of their lives that they get used to and unintentionally don't want it to go away. But it takes courage to let the hurt know that it's game over for it, to stand face to face with the hurt and politely ask it to buzz off. It doesn't take courage to stay hurt, but it takes a hell lot of courage to let go of it and choose happiness.

My villagers were fighters in that respect—true courageous fighters. Uncle Deva was the spark of hope and the pillar of support for them. I wondered what it took for him to be this way. Courage? Bravery?

I watched the women of the village wear their fancy sarees and cook pongal in their mud pots. The ground was filled with rangoli designs. The kids had also taken part. They had scribbled in their scrawny handwriting in the rangoli saying, 'Welcome home Deva uncle'.

I swallowed back a lump in my throat. I instantly reflected on the moment when I had said that the kids liked Vijay because he brought gifts. The children understood intentions far better than us.

After the hubbub died down a bit, uncle Deva had a few minutes to sit on a stone to gaze at his people smiling. Me and Aadhi sat near him.

"What next?" Asked Aadhi. "Vijay under arrest. Case with CBI. You think everything will turn out okay, dad?"

"No way," was the reply.

"What?" I squealed.

"They won't give us peace that easily. Releasing me, arresting Vijay, handing over this case to CBI are just like biscuits you throw to the dog to stop it from barking; not to satisfy the hunger."

"That's rude," I said.

"You don't know Vijay, Shrav!" he said, "That man is one ruthless being. You think he would let his empire crumble that easily?"

"Or let another person use the chair his ass rested on!" Aadhi added.

Silence lingered for the next two minutes.

"I'm scared," I said. "Really scared. What if…"

He looked at me and smiled and pulled my head in for a kiss on my forehead.

"Are you worried something will happen to me? I'm made of iron, my girl! I won't die before I make those duffers rot in hell!"

Aadhi hugged his father's arm forlornly. I hugged his other one. Uncle Deva opened his arm and pulled us close to his chest and held us tight. I knew the smile on his face had faded. I couldn't see his face, but I felt it. Maybe he was scared too; not because of the lurking danger, but probably because he feared he might fail his people.

To tell you the truth, I had a feeling that he was harbouring something deep; something else was bothering him, which was pushing him to fight against Veera Explosives. Something else that was making him take this fight personally. I did not know if it was true or just my instinct, but I just felt it.

The day went well. Everyone took their turn in feeding uncle Deva the tastily cooked food—one by one, one or two mouthfuls, including the kids, as they thought that he was barely fed in the jail. I thought his stomach might just pop, but he took in all their food and love. He looked at me and sighed wearily.

I knew in that moment that he was one of the few people I could love from the bottom of my heart in this lifetime. Uncle Deva. His name always sent a vibration of respect, of love, of hope. He saw me looking intently at him and threw a smile. I planted the biggest kiss on his cheek.

25
THE PHONE CALL

11 February 2017
Coimbatore

I had come back to Coimbatore now that things had died down. I missed Aadhi. I had spent a lot of time with him, mostly in trauma, which had made the lack of his presence extremely hard. I had become used to having him around. I wanted to pour out everything that happened at school—the exciting and mundane things—to Aadhi, but I stayed away from him.

I did not know what was happening in the village and I didn't want him to listen to my stories when I had no idea of his current mindset. Uncle Deva, however, called me every day! He never got bored with listening to my stories. I was glad I had at least one person to share everything.

My dad was a reputed Vastu consultant in Coimbatore. You might not know this, but the city of Coimbatore is filled with rich Gounders who believe in everything that sounds supernatural, yet based on science. They have a knack for fantasy, but they need it to stand on solid ground. However, they are smart. They can tell real talents and pick apart frauds very easily.

My dad's way with people, coupled with his knowledge of Vastu and seamlessly merging construction and Vastu scientifically, made his approach very likeable and interesting. In turn, it had also made him famous.

It was one of those days that a Gounder businessman had invited him to take a look at one of his old mansions. It was situated in Sulur, deep in the suburbs. My dad picked up on vibes. He could tell if something bad had happened in a place the moment he stepped inside a building. Consider it uncanny or too good to be true, but I had seen him once telling a client directly that the woman of the house—the one the client had introduced as his wife—was not, in fact, his wife. The ashamed client begged him to tell how he had figured that out. Dad replied that the Vastu of the house was in such a way that the actual woman of this house either had to be dead or overseas.

I had no idea how he did that. There were a lot of such instances which I loved hearing about when he came back home after a consultation, especially when he visited houses like these.

And now an old mansion, untouched, in the middle of the woods. How much more interesting could it get? My dad peeled the groundnuts and gave it to me and my mom as he narrated the story.

Apparently, dad had felt the presence of a girl who had died in the house by hanging herself. The moment he stepped inside the mansion, he had felt the girl wail, though he did not see any ghostly form. The south-west of the house, which is meant to be the solidity of the house, had been degraded by using it as a storage room. He also felt a strong pull towards the well that was situated at the back of the house. Dad had immediately called his client over and asked him what had really happened in the house, and if there had been a woman who had committed suicide. Shocked, the Gounder had started crying saying that this mansion had once been his home and that it had been his mother who passed away by hanging when he was a kid. Since then, his father hadn't allowed him to sell the property, but recently, after his death, the client had decided to sell it out, and that's why the Vastu consultation.

"I told him directly that you can't sell this place." Dad said, munching the groundnuts.

"Woah!" I said.

"The soul has connected itself to that house. And the entire Vastu of the house is wrong for it to have any hope."

I listened in awe.

"When the Vastu is wrong, forces that are supernatural have more powers."

I nodded fast, as if I understood every word.

Dad's mobile rang, interrupting my thought process. That was when I realized I had my mouth open all this while.

"It's Rudran," Dad said and picked up the phone. I checked the time randomly. It was 1 a.m. No wonder I was feeling drowsy.

I came to the kitchen to drink water. As I was drinking, I heard my father repeatedly saying 'what', each *what* increasing in pitch and sound, the last one breaking as if my dad was crying. I dropped the tumbler and ran into the hall.

My dad was down on the ground, holding the phone in one hand and his chest in the other and was crying, while my mother rubbed his shoulders and begged him to tell what was wrong. My pulse quickened and my mind threw up various scenarios in a moment. I went by my dad's side and held him. The call had ended and he let the mobile drop.

"Tell me. What happened? Why are you crying?" My mother started crying too. Not even a drop escaped my eyes, but I knew I had forgotten to blink or swallow.

"D-Deva," my dad muttered in between sobs and my whole world swirled. I saw black.

"What? What happened?" My mother asked continuously, but I already knew the reply. I just wanted to somehow shut out dad's next words, and my body was paralysed.

"Deva was murdered. They stabbed him so many times..." my dad's voice broke again but he managed to speak. "His body was found on the rock below the hill that we went to on Aadhi's birthday. Come on. We have to go."

26
FINE LINE

Something told me it was a lie. Though pain and tears were gushing out of me, I suppressed them because it *had* to be wrong. Who could hurt uncle Deva, and how *could* he die? How could he leave us behind? Our moments together at the rock near the well, our swimming sessions, his smile, the scar on his temple…

Something cracked inside me. My aunt and uncle, who lived close by, had joined us in the car to go to Achipatti. My aunt sat beside me and was constantly crying. My mind had gone blank. My dad had asked his friend to come to drive us as he could not drive under these circumstances.

Nothing was wrong because the information clearly was false. It had to be. Deva uncle was fine. He was probably in the hospital with a few stitches. Rudran uncle might have freaked out and called dad. He could never handle a thing without my dad. That was it. I breathed.

I wondered how it was just a thin line between extreme relief and extreme grief. Why is it so? Why did God create situations in such a way that one word, one instance, one word of truth, can either be the biggest source of relief or turn our world upside down to an extent that we can't ever get back up?

Why is it always a fine line? Why can't it be a broad way? Why don't we have the luxury of breaking down our grief and placing it in the width of the broad way so that we heal better?

Why do things always have to be either black or white? Why can't they be shades of grey?

I wanted to call uncle Deva and ask him directly. But what if he didn't pick? A chill solidified in my stomach. No. I wasn't that brave. Though I knew something was wrong, my mind hated to accept it.

Denial. Ever tried it? Works wonders.

I still remember my denial. Why do we have to know the truth? Our idea of truth in the head is good enough. Why know the actual truth that could rip us apart if we have the luxury of denial that could save our soul like a charm?!

I controlled my urge to call Aadhi. No. That was risky, too.

What if his voice broke? What if he said the worst? Nope. I had to be there to nurse my uncle back to health. Yeah, that was it. The moment I was near him, he would be fine. I felt slightly better.

I don't remember if I was praying or crying or was paralysed in the next hour. I had no idea. My aunt's weeping noise that was ringing in my ears faded away slowly as I disappeared into nothingness. I knew we were headed to the hospital. There we were going to find out that nothing was wrong. I was sure I was going to beat the hell out of Deva uncle the moment I met him. I waited.

The car turned into a driveway. I immediately opened the door and ran out. There was no hospital. It was too dark, and in the midst of it, I saw a crackling light. A light on a board. The board that said *Mortuary.*

My stomach twisted. My eyes widened, and I kept rereading the board in spite of the hanging cobwebs.

No. No.

"No!!!" I screamed. My family looked at me. "We are in the wrong place. We are in the wrong place. This isn't the hospital! Take me to the hospital!"

I broke down on the ground, the sharp sting from the pebble jamming into my knee feeling like a tickle. I saw the blurred figure of my mother running towards me. But suddenly, a pair of strong hands lifted me up from behind. I arched my neck with difficulty. My vision blurred again the instant I laid my eyes on that face.

"Aadhi!" I screamed. "Aadhi. It's not true, is it? Why are you at the mortuary? Let's go to the hospital. No. Let's go home. He will be there."

Aadhi was silent. I did not want to look at his face. My brain listened to me immediately by blurring my vision because once I took in his countenance, I would know the actual truth, and that was the last thing I wanted. Rudran uncle came running to us, caught hold of my dad, held him tight and took him to the back of the grim building. I was about to follow them.

Aadhi held my hand tight. I still did not look at his face. He smelled of soil and sweat and something unfamiliar. Something raw and metallic. I blinked the blur away and looked at his T-shirt.

Blood stains.

My heart felt a punch. My dad and uncle Rudran came out from behind, this time my dad with his hand on his chest, weeping. At that moment, I knew.

The truth had hit me, not gently, not slowly, but with the intensity and force of a tornado, knocking me over. Aadhi tied his kerchief around my bleeding knee. I looked at him. His face was tired, his eyes red and his mouth twitching from controlling the sobs. I hugged him tight and wept at the bloodstain on his chest.

And still, amidst the metallic odour, I could inhale Deva uncle's fragrance. The one I felt when I hugged him at the station. The one fragrance that always gave me comfort. My legs gave way and together me and Aadhi crashed on the ground.

I did not know what happened in the next two days. Everything happened so quickly. The whole village arrived at his house that night, and the roars I heard the other day turned into even louder cries. It was like their most favourite family member had passed. It seemed Constable Syed had collapsed when he heard the news. I heard from my parents that he had a mild cardiac arrest and that he was in the hospital getting treatment. He had been so close to uncle Deva—looked up to him, loved him, got inspired by him for years. No wonder he had crumbled.

I heard the wails growing louder. They brought him wrapped in white—his tall body, the stone abs, the fit body now so vulnerable and weak. Anger surged through me to an extent that I felt nauseous. I felt something metallic in my mouth. That's when I realised I had chewed my lip. I wiped the blood off. How dare they make him this way? How dare they make my rock crumble like this? What right did they have to make a good man of honour as lifeless and fragile as a butterfly's wing?

They put him on a table and the entire village ran towards him to give their final kisses and touch him for one last time. I felt weak when I pushed my way amongst them to reach him. That's when I saw his face. I had to. Because I was never going to see it again. There were no marks on his face, thank God. He still looked brave and his mouth curved as though he was smiling, but his adorable eyes were shut. I felt a stab at my chest. His face didn't look as weak or vulnerable as his body was. I touched his cheek and forehead and something inside me cracked. His skin felt strangely cold and unearthly. Not the usual warm and sweaty.

Tears poured down my face. My eyes moved to the tiny scar on his temple. The one he had always told me he had got while fighting a tiger. I ran my finger over it, as I always used to, the ragged skin which always made me laugh, as I knew it came from his fall off the bed when he was a kid. Now even that scar seemed different, lifeless. I wept and wept and there was nobody there to hold me or help me. Because they were equally helpless. The scar danced in front of me, multiplying into two. And then four. They moved and danced like a wave and I blinked my eyes. Everything was dark. I didn't know what happened next, but I heard a thud.

I wanted uncle Deva to calm me down and hug me. Only him and no one else.

It's funny how the worst kind of pain is actually caused by the *only* person we want to comfort us during the worst kind of pain. Ironic, right? But turns out, when that pain appears, they are never available. We have to deal with it ourselves.

I knew I had fainted. I thought when I woke up, things would be different. They weren't. The first thing I heard when I woke up was the drum sounds during the funeral, which lingered in my memories for the next few days. We did nothing. We just stayed at uncle Deva's place, slept, cried, ate and repeated the cycle. Aadhi, though he wanted to be alone and immersed in his grief, stayed by my side but never uttered a word.

An incident like this was exactly what he was afraid of, and I had called him a coward for that. I wanted to apologize and hug him and utter words of comfort. But I realized nothing would ever comfort him, so I stayed silent.

Our family was shattered, and so was the village. Inspector Rajendran arrived the next morning with a smug look on his face to conduct the investigation. I wanted to punch him, boil his skin, tear his smiling mouth and pluck out those eyes that kept rolling. But I kept quiet. I wished Deva uncle was with me. He'd have known what exactly to do at a time like this. And every time that thought emerged, I broke down and cried.

We filed a complaint against the factory, claiming that they were the reason for his murder, especially mentioning Vijay's name. But the inspector threw the letter of complaint on the table saying that Vijay was in CBI custody and that it was foolish of us to doubt him.

"Obviously he hired someone," I said. "A hitman. I doubt a man of his power would get his hands dirty."

Aadhi was shocked at my rebuke and shushed me. The inspector kept glaring at me.

We knew in an instant that the police proceedings that happened later were just an eyewash. The media, somehow, did not utter a word about his murder. Aadhi tried calling that reporter that made him famous through that Live. She did not respond, and even blocked his calls! Every media outlet turned deaf ears to our loudest cry. Slowly, the blast issue also faded from the TV.

All of this happened within a week, and we had no idea how. How was this sudden change possible?

"Vijay Kumar," Aadhi uttered, "He has shut everyone up. Especially the one that had the loudest voice. My dad."

27
DETAILS

A Month Later

My menstrual cycle repeated itself twice because of the unrecognized stress I went through. His loss was inexplicably hard on me, mostly because I kept denying it. I just believed he would walk in the door any time, speaking about a new issue in the village, or suddenly asking me to get ready for swimming, or sprint out of the kitchen with a bowl of curd in his hands to feed me. None of it happened.

All these feelings have passed now. I wouldn't say completely passed, but faded. Faded with time. The pain we think is permanent has a tendency to fade. That doesn't mean you would heal completely; that never happens. But the intensity certainly depletes as we learn to shove it aside and bury it.

It was then that I began asking what really happened that night—the night of the murder. All this while, I had no strength to do so. The time of death was around 12:30 a.m. What was he doing up at the hill so late at night? He wouldn't be up late unless he was working on something important. And what was he working on if the blast case was already being taken care of by the CBI? Why would uncle Deva go to that hill in the dead of the night? Why would Aadhi not accompany him?

"He got a phone call from an unknown number while he was having dinner," Aadhi said.

"Who was that?"

"I have no idea."

"The police must have traced the number, right? Clearly, they wouldn't help us. Shall we try to find out by other means?"

"Done already. I have asked one of my friends from college to hack into dad's phone and find out who called, and find any other details from it."

"But the phone is in the evidence locker," I said. "How will he do it?"

"I stole it," he hung his head low.

"What?" I jumped.

"That's the least I could do. It wasn't that hard. When the police were collecting his personal belongings, I stole it. Just grabbed it when no one was looking. They created a big issue out of it, but I think they blamed each other for being careless and forgot about it."

"Good. Good."

"Good?"

"Yeah, you did something illegal for your dad. How am I going to blame you? You have all my support."

He nodded.

"Anyway, did your friend find anything yet?"

"Not yet."

"Any idea what the person who called spoke about?"

"Don't know what they said on the other end. But he got very agitated and said he had to leave."

"Why didn't you stop him?" I asked.

"I should have," he said and made his hand into a fist and beat his chest. That question was a stab at his heart. "I should have. But I didn't. Because it wasn't unusual for him to leave suddenly without telling me where he was going. So…" He paused.

"I'm sorry," I said. I didn't reach out to him. It felt risky.

"I thought it was one of those nights. Where he leaves without telling me and comes back in the morning. I had no idea…" he buried his face into his palms.

"Aadhi," I moved towards him. "Look at me. It's not your mistake."

"What if it is?"

I had no answer for that.

"You can't blame yourself for it. For a question that you're never going to find the answer for."

He stayed silent.

"We have to find out who did this." I said, my eyes slowly tearing up. He looked at me, his sadness fading and his temper rising. His eyes slowly started growing red. "We do," I repeated. "Let's rewind. Find out all the details. Every single one. We have to ruin whoever did this. We should show them what it's like to burn in hell."

We decided to take a walk. It was around 10:30 p.m. The crime scene had been trodden over so many times by the police and the locals. There was no use going back to it again. But something wanted me to. Maybe we would find something that the police had missed. The police were bound to miss it anyway—intentionally bound.

"Let's go to the hill," I said, and Aadhi looked at me as if he had been shot.

"What?"

"Let's go. We might find something."

"Shravya, whatever there was worth finding, would have already been confiscated by the police to remove evidence. They are against us, remember?"

"What if they missed something?"

"It happened a month ago. A month! What can we expect to find now?"

My heart fell. He was right.

"Let's just go."

I hadn't realized it might be a traumatic experience for Aadhi. It was wrong on my part, but Deva uncle was gone. Whatever we did now wasn't going to bring him back. The least we could do was to try to avenge his death. I had reached that place in my thoughts, but Aadhi sure wouldn't have. It was his dad, his hero. Avenging his death would probably come later on, not just one month after. Also, going to the one place in which he had one of the best memories with his father would literally rip his heart out. I wondered why someone would kill him there. My blood grew stale, and I grew nauseous.

Aadhi agreed to come for my sake. He must have loved me that much. We had parottas for dinner at the parotta stand, but this time without a word, without eye contact. It was tasty, but I didn't care as long as it filled my empty stomach. After that, we started walking towards the hill as the silent chilly winds blew. The dropping temperature did not bother us as our insides grew even colder with every step we took towards the hill. We reached the foot of the hill and started climbing, still without a word.

* * *

I had taken the trip to the top of the hill umpteen times, but none of the times were as excruciating as this. It all boiled down to that, right? When our minds collapse, even the easiest, most loved task becomes the most painful thing to do. Though it might say on billboards and self-help books and magazines that health determines everything, your health, no matter how fit you are, would just flutter away if your mind is shattered. Physical and mental health are deeply intertwined like milk and water, and it takes more than just a swan to separate them. Maybe spirituality is all about that. Being a swan. Dividing your health, mind, career, dream, emotions into different segments, and learning to react and work on them one segment at a time is probably what meditation teaches you about. It takes a lot of maturity and discipline to mould ourselves to divide. We know it all. We have theories on how to do things, but when it comes to applying what we talk about to ourselves, we gloriously fail.

My thoughts were interrupted by a groan. I turned around to see Aadhi on his knees. He had slipped. He did not roll off because the hill wasn't that steep. It was a place where even toddlers won't slip, let alone a fit, healthy person like Aadhi. He had no divisions or segments in his head to separate his health from the shallows of his mind. I helped him up and, without looking at his face, I climbed up.

We had reached the summit, and the moon shone beautifully. Again, the mind made us overlook its beauty.

"There," Aadhi said and pointed to my right. I saw police tapes. My heart froze. We walked towards it for minutes. Guess we both took the smallest and slowest steps possible. The tapes marked the edge of the hill. I gazed past the edge, into the valley. There was a big rock right below the edge.

It wasn't visible clearly as the shadow of the edge made the rock pitch black. I kept looking as my eyes adjusted. It was then I saw it. The surface of the rock.

And splotches of something dark on it here and there. My eyes widened as a lightning of terror darted through me, solidifying into an aching numbness in my stomach.

It was blood. Uncle Deva's blood. That was where the body had been dumped, according to dad. I turned to Aadhi, pulling him away. Too late. He had already seen it. I knew from his face. It was blank. In a second, he broke down on his knees.

I did not stop him or reach out to him. He did not weep. He was just silent, his breath wheezy. I let it happen. It should. I looked away. I tried to divide. I tried to push my emotions into one segment and my sanity into the other. It was excruciating, but I somehow managed to push an ounce of my shock into the segment as I tried looking for a path to reach the stone and look near it, to find something, anything. There were no paths. We could reach only by jumping, which was impossible considering the rock was pulled in from the edge. If we jumped, we would land in the valley and die.

I looked as Aadhi's wheezy breaths sent slivers of agony down my spine. The sand near the edge was scuffled and thrown about as if there had been a struggle. When I looked clearly, there was blood everywhere.

Even in the place we stood. It was then that I saw it. The huge banyan tree that was a few metres away from the edge on the right. Me and uncle Deva has visited this hill a lot of times after Aadhi's birthday and we used to sit under this tree, eating snacks from my backpack. Tears rolled down my cheek. I went towards the tree and sat underneath it. There was no one on my side and it ached. Not a stinging sharp ache, but a dull, heavy pain wearing me down into the mud. I grabbed the ground in pain. I wept and wept and kept grabbing the ground, trying to transfer my pain to the ground. Trying to earth it, literally.

It was then that something pricked my arm. I looked down and opened my palm. It was a crushed piece of thin paper, almost buried under the mud. My constant grabbing at the soil must have unearthed the paper. Must be a cigarette box, I thought. It was then that I saw something scribbled in it.

I opened it. It was a passport-size photo. Of a girl.

Something sent a shudder down my spine, and I did not know why. I did know what it was, but the shudder chilled me with each passing second. Sometimes our instinct really picks out and projects certain things that we have no rational explanations of. This was one such moment.

I straightened the picture to get a better view.

I wondered who it was, but the first thought that came to mind was that she was breathtakingly beautiful. I could make it out despite a hundred creases in the picture. The passport photo seemed too old and worn out, as if it was many years old, at least a decade. I gazed at it for a minute. How did this come here? Who was she? And why did I get the inexplicable shudder?

It was then I remembered seeing something scribbled on the back. I turned it around. In a scrawny handwriting, it was written:

Archana Deva

My blood froze.

28

WANT TO STAB ME? AIM FOR MY CHEST, NEVER MY BACK

I couldn't sleep that night. I kept glancing at the picture, at her lovely face and asking myself why she had written her and uncle Deva's names together. Was she his secret daughter? Nah, Deva uncle couldn't have a daughter this big. I did not show the picture to Aadhi. He was already grieving. The visit to the scene of the crime had been a bit much for him to handle. I could only imagine what he was going through, and whatever I could have done wouldn't have changed a thing. I didn't want to confuse him on top of that.

Moreover, the shudder I felt when I laid my eyes on the picture felt too personal. Too *mine*. I felt like I had to find the truth and not share it with anyone. Maybe it was nothing. Maybe it was some other Deva. Maybe the picture had fallen out of someone's bag by mistake when they visited the temple on the hill.

Dang.

The more theories I came up with, the more they seemed pointless. They were constantly being proven wrong in my head by that one shudder I couldn't shake off.

I suddenly thought of Syed.

Syed had been with uncle Deva for a long time. He stuck around pretty much since the time uncle Deva had started helping people. He might know who this girl was. Tomorrow, I had to visit him in the hospital. I closed my eyes and slipped into a deep slumber. I had no idea how it happened. How hours of chaos and sleeplessness vanished in a jiffy when one clear thought popped up.

"Shravya! Wake up!" I heard Aadhi call my name continually and nudge me in the most ruthless way.

"You're a pain in the ass. Go away!" I screamed.

"Shravya, we know who called dad."

He should not have done that. He shouldn't have quoted sentences that would give me an instant cardiac arrest when I was not in my right mind. It didn't, thanks to my health. But it did give a damning headache.

"What?"

"We know who called dad last." He was sweating. It didn't seem good.

"Someone we know?" I asked slowly, clutching my head. "Vijay?"

"No."

"Who is it?"

"I can't believe it," Aadhi sat on the bed, clutching his head.

"Just tell me."

He looked at me and gave this stabbed look.

"Who?" I asked.

"It's Syed."

I felt the ground beneath me shake.

* * *

I couldn't hold it in any longer. I showed Aadhi the passport size picture. He had no idea who that girl was, and the scribbling behind it shocked him. We headed to the hospital where Syed was admitted. We had to take the bus to Pollachi. We debated whether to tell my parents, but decided against it. Involving the elders would just create more drama and fewer results, and sure, a hell lot of answering to do. Especially by Aadhi for stealing. And then a lot of bickering about this and that—about how they couldn't believe Syed would do this, and how someone would say that they already felt that vibe about him but decided to keep it quiet. Elders, drama and their urge to look down upon the kids were a combination made in heaven.

"How did your guy find out?" I asked. "Did Syed call from his mobile? If so, why did it take him one month to find?"

"The call came from a burner phone."

"I thought burners are untraceable."

"They are. But every call, every text, every exchange goes through a cell phone provider."

"And your guy got another guy in there?" I asked. "Who helped your guy?"

"Kind of. I mean, people owe people sometimes. We all have people we owe to. It's not a big deal. This was something like that."

I thought about how his words played out.

"Blackmail?" I asked. "Your guy had dirt on the guy at the cell phone provider?"

"Uh, maybe," Aadhi said. "Let's not get into the details of that."

He shushed me.

"You're full of crap. Too sleazy. I like this version of you better than the righteous, strict one," I said with a smile.

"Maybe I was always like this. Grief just pushed me off the edge."

I turned silent. I wished this pain didn't change Aadhi for the worse. Pain had the ability to turn a man wise or wounded, as the yogis put it. And from the way Aadhi was behaving, I was sure he was having fluctuating reactions to being wounded. I held his arm tightly and rested my head on his shoulder. He caressed my hair and rested his head on top of mine. Tears emerged effortlessly from my eyes. Whether he turned out wise or wounded, I knew one thing wouldn't change. He wouldn't stop loving me and neither would I.

The bus turned into the Pollachi bus stand. We had heard the elders mention that Syed was in JP hospital. We took an auto there, headed to the reception and asked for Syed. The receptionist began checking her logbook.

It was after I mentioned his name that I realized the sudden blow that came along with it. We trusted Syed anna for pretty much everything. He was the reason Deva uncle was taken care of at the station. He had been with us through thick and thin, and now to think he was the last person who called uncle Deva before he died?

I swallowed hard.

"You okay?" the receptionist asked.

"Y-Yeah. Just a parched throat."

She nodded. "One Syed Ibrahim, admitted for chest pains?"

"Yes," Aadhi said, eyeing me.

"He is in ward 2. Sign here and you can visit him."

We sauntered into the ward. The gatch beds lay grudgingly with even more grudging patients on them. Hospitals always give off a whiff of depression—unavoidable, sudden draught in the air, a knot in the stomach. The vibe wears you down. I held on to Aadhi.

In the gatch bed, the one before last, lay Syed. Well, he actually sat with his back resting on the worn-out pillow, his eyes gazing into nothingness, his face forlorn. Anger surged within me. If he had got something to do with uncle Deva's murder, I'd punch him to death. Aadhi held my hand and raced me to Syed's bed.

He didn't even look at us until we approached his bed, and the moment he laid his eyes on us, it was like he had just been in an earthquake. He jumped out of his skin, literally.

Frankly, we had thought that his calling Uncle Deva in the end was a coincidence, and that a man like Syed would have nothing to do with his death. But looking at his reaction now, we knew we were clearly wrong to have trusted Syed. Dara Shikoh, indeed! This man was an embodiment of the murderous younger brother. The anger made me numb.

Got a heart attack, my ass! This guy had murdered my uncle.

"Don't you dare dream about running, you sick son of a bitch,"

Aadhi said to him in a low, calm voice, holding the steel rod of the gatch bed with more force than necessary.

"W-what?" he said with his face aghast.

The more scared he looked, the angrier we got. "You were the last person who called appa," Aadhi said. "After that call, he went out somewhere and got murdered."

He looked away, his breaths turning shallow. Syed was a cheerful, handsome man. He always looked so focussed, like he was always thinking about something or the other. He loosened up only when he was with uncle Deva. When he first became a police officer, the first person he reached out to share the news with was uncle Deva.

Deva uncle, in turn, had hugged him tight and revealed the news to the rest of the villagers, who celebrated Syed that night by cooking food and sharing. We never really had anything against him. Deva uncle considered him like a brother. How could he?

"How could you?" Aadhi asked with so much pain in his voice that I swallowed hard.

"Look," Syed started. His lips were turning dry. "You don't know what happened."

"Tell us."

"I can't," he said. "It's complicated."

"What the heck?" Aadhi raised his voice, and the rest of the patients began murmuring. I held his hand tight.

"Complicated?" I asked in a lower voice. "Tell us or I'll tell my dad and every person in Achipatti. Imagine what would happen if they knew you had something to do with uncle's murder? They'll beat you to death."

"No. Please," Syed said. "I did not murder bhai. How would I? I'd rather be dead." He started crying. I had never seen him cry before, so I didn't know if his tears were fake or real.

"Then what did you do?" I asked.

"I-uh-just called him."

"Why?"

His eyes turned red.

"I can't say," he said and leaned towards us. "They'll kill me."

"Who?" Aadhi asked, clutching the iron rod tighter.

"Who do you think?"

"Vijay?"

"It's complicated."

"Did they blackmail you?" Aadhi narrowed his eyes.

He stayed silent.

"They did. Didn't they?"

My mind raced. "Your sister, where is she?" I asked.

Again, he gave that deathly pale look. I was right. It had something to do with his sister.

"Did they kidnap your sister in return for a favour?"

He buried his face in his palms and wept. "Yes."

Aadhi sat on the gatch bed, grabbed the man's hand and pulled it open to reveal his face.

"Tell me everything. Do not leave out a word. And don't say the word 'complicated' again or you're done for."

"They kidnapped my sister. You know she's spastic. They threatened to kill her if I didn't do as they said."

"And what was that?"

"I was supposed to call Deva bhai from a burner. Tell him that I'm in trouble. That the Veera Explosives gang were chasing me up the hill."

"And why would they do that?"

"They were angry with the police for nailing Vijay. As I was close to bhai, they were trying to kill me."

"So, this is what you were supposed to say to appa," Aadhi said, holding back his tears, "to lure him to the hill."

"Yes," Syed said, again weeping into his palms.

"You know who killed him?" I asked. "You know who was on the hill that night?"

"I have no idea. I called him from my home, as I was panicking."

You cheap son of a -

My thoughts were cut short as Aadhi spoke.

"You think Vijay committed the murder himself? Or was it others from the factory?"

"Vijay is in CBI custody, right? He couldn't have come here."

"Who called you and told you your sister was kidnapped? You remember the voice?"

"It was robotic. As if it was manipulated by some AI."

"You are a police officer yourself," I said. "How long would it take for you to start a police operation and nail those bastards?"

"It's not that easy. My superiors are all corrupt. They would immediately side with Vijay. I couldn't pull it off alone. I was s-scared."

"So you let him die," I said point blank. "Whatever the situation you were in, you let him die. You will forever carry his blood on your hands."

My eyes turned teary, and seeing him so vulnerable increased my anger multifold. How could he just sit there like a kitten and cry after pulling off a selfish scam to save himself and his loved one using my uncle as bait?

"How dare you?" I asked, wiping the tears. "How dare you? This world would be a better place without scared people like you. If Deva uncle were in your position, he would have gone to any extent to save you. This world needs fearless people like him. And because of useless ones like you, he was slaughtered," I paused to swallow. "How dare you?"

He was growing smaller and smaller with each word, and I didn't care. He should disappear in guilt, and I should watch him do so.

"Calm down, Shravya," Aadhi said. "Just be calm."

"Are you taking his side?"

"Circumstances would push a man to do anything."

"What the..."

"Did you get your sister back?" Aadhi asked.

"Yes."

"Is your heart attack even real?" I asked.

"Yes." He said, and in an instant, I knew he was telling the truth. I wouldn't say I saw it in his eyes or cliché crap like that. I just knew. It hit me.

"You did not expect that they would kill him," I said. "You just thought they were going to threaten him. Or blackmail him. Or something else. But not murder."

He wept.

"So, you cracked when you knew that Deva uncle was murdered," I said.

"Which means he was true to appa," Aadhi said. "He was true. Circumstances pushed him to do so."

"Whatever it is, I can never forgive him," I paused.

"You don't have to," Syed said. "I can't forgive myself. Ever."

"And that's your biggest punishment," I said.

Alright, so one thing is solved. Syed was blackmailed into calling uncle Deva. We didn't know who exactly asked him to call, except it was someone from Veera Explosives. Hence, obviously, Vijay was behind it. Whoever called did according to his order. I had one more thing to ask Syed. I reached into my purse and pulled out the straightened passport size picture.

"Do you know who this is?" I asked.

The face is the mirror of the soul; they say. At that moment, I just knew his soul had cracked. All this while, his face expressed fear, guilt, denial, etc. But at that moment, I couldn't quite fathom which emotion he was going through, but I knew it was a mixture of all the emotions and something beyond. He tried to hide it so well that his face stayed almost blank. No expression at all. But I saw the tiny twitching of his left eye, a sudden jerk in his cheek and the minute twisting of his thin lips.

Bottom line—he knew her.

I waited. He looked up at me. This time, the fear was all gone. It was just a look that said nothing, absolutely nothing. The way one looks at a stranger—without any thought or intention—just one plain glance that says nothing. That's how he looked at me. And for a second, it startled me.

"Do not touch this," he said, again without any expression. That took me aback. Even Aadhi moved slightly away from the man. The tears weren't even dry on his face, but his countenance had metamorphosed to the extreme opposite. Even if he had gotten scared or angry to the core, it wouldn't have scared me this much. Only the epitome of an emotion can lead to the peak of numbness, the peak of blankness, of nothingness. If a man is exposed to extreme pain, he turns numb and too powerful. Because he has nothing to lose. And all I saw on Syed's face was numbness.

"What do you mean?" I whispered.

"Do not touch this," he repeated, his voice hard. The air around us turned chilly.

"I don't understand. Why? Who is she?"

"Forbidden," he said. "Talking about her is forbidden."

"By whom?"

"Well," he paused and looked away. "It's, uh, complicated."

29
A SURPRISE VISIT

18 October 2019

Two years had passed. Nothing significant had happened in these two years. Even after I knew for sure that Syed was hiding something about the woman in the picture, I couldn't do anything.

We can't always have our ways no matter how much we want, and that's the raw truth. We can really plan things out to the last detail, but life always has the habit of slapping you hard and forcing you to take another direction, urging you to look away. Though we have a driving force that is more important than life itself, still we look away because, well, life happens, humbling us all the way down.

What urged me to look away? Nothing. I didn't look away. I didn't want to but I was made to do so, or so I tell myself. Vijay Kumar, who was under the scrutiny of the CBI and the police, was set free because the police had failed to file the charge sheet within ninety days. Reasons. Excuses. Loopholes. CBI had been an eyewash, and we felt like fools to have believed that they would have done something. Money played the role of a powerful, dominant wife, while justice was the pitied mistress that everyone laughed at.

The factory stayed open, in spite of everything. With a phenomenal hike in the salary, people from families other than the victims' were eager to work there. Only the victims' families held the wrath and the grudge and overlooked money. The rest chose money because they did not have a personal crisis. The world operated that way, sadly. This caused a lot of tension in the village. Fights worse than bar brawls happened on the streets. Families who ate and slept together stood up against each other and called each other names. Integrated, loving families of the village became fragmented and greed-filled.

Without uncle Deva, things fell apart.

Or maybe the departing of uncle Deva was an excuse for the villagers to go back to who they really were. Maybe uncle Deva just triggered the goodness in them that would have never seen the light of day had it not been for him.

The fertility of the village was slowly deteriorating. The water table was slowly turning dark, the cattle were getting sick, and the villagers were getting diseases that the village doctor couldn't name.

However, they all stayed quiet because the money inflow was excellent. Money had shut them up. As for uncle Deva's murder, the case was finally picked up by the police seriously after advocate Madhav Kumar decided to back it up. This was the same man I had met—uncle Deva's brother-in-law, who loathed him for his sister's murder.

Still, no progress on the case. The police gave us a hard time while they pretended to go ahead with the case.

Dad got busy with his work. I got busy with school and so did Aadhi. Life moved on, grudgingly, and we unintentionally decided to overlook uncle Deva and his life's mission, though we loved him very much. Our visits to the village drastically reduced because it was so depressing to see everything changing. It happens, right? Suddenly, when we wake up one day and the one thing that is the most important to us doesn't seem that way. We just get up and move on.

The media decided to bury the blast case. Vijay's money floated around and shut everyone up. Health Minister Kalingaraj visited the village regularly every month to butter the people more with his tactics and money. Hell, people even started supporting his party. Some even offered to work for his party. Dumb people. How could they do that even after uncle Deva lost his life fighting for them?

Frankly, we weren't as determined as uncle Deva. We just let it happen. My dad just told me in the morning that the Veera Explosives guys had filed a petition requesting the court to withdraw the case on them due to the blast. It was outrageous to know that the court was even considering it. Their NOC was cancelled after the blast when uncle Deva pushed for it, but it was again brought back—well, *bought back*—after his death. We were powerless to fight against it and the cruellest thing was; we were okay with being so.

The petition for withdrawal of charges, however, angered my father.

"What can we do?" my dad asked.

"I have no idea."

"I'm going to Achipatti. Let me speak with the people and the police, see what I can do."

My heart fluttered. It had been almost a year since I last saw Aadhi. We had lost contact. He became busy with balancing his part-time work and studies. He had no one to support him. My dad tried a lot of times to take care of him, but Aadhi declined politely.

"Can I come along?" I asked, half hoping dad would decline. He didn't.

"Sure. It would be a nice change for you."

I wished Aadhi would be there. Last I had heard was that he had moved to Chennai to pursue his work and studies there. Uncle Deva's land and home still remained uninhabited, and word was that Aadhi stayed there alone whenever he visited the village, which was rare.

You must be wondering what happened to Syed. Well, the uncanny visit at the hospital—that was the last time I ever laid eyes on him. I heard from dad that he had quit his job and had left the village with his sister. He had disappeared, obviously. I could just sigh at the news. I knew why, but there was no use ratting him out to the elders. Obviously, he was blackmailed into doing that heinous job of luring uncle. But his reaction regarding the girl in the picture was strange indeed. Still, I didn't want to talk about it to anyone. I just let it pass. Not to mention the fact that there were nights I woke up drenched in sweat due to nightmares where the pretty girl from the picture would come running to strangle me and to stab uncle Deva. Why would she choose two methods of killing? I had no idea. And then Syed's blank face cut right through the scene and told me, "It's complicated".

It was all weird. I had the windows down as dad sped his way to Achipatti. Each passing second made my heart leap. I prayed I wouldn't meet Aadhi, and then I prayed harder that I would. Then I decided not to pray at all, and turned the stereo to its full volume, getting occasional yelling from my dad.

We reached Rudran uncle's home in no time. He pulled dad in for a big hug and then me, and said the usual stuff about me having grown up a lot, etc. My eyes searched for Aadhi, but I couldn't find him. The house was filled with my aunty's presence and nothingness. A void that was too heavy, sheathed with pain. Deva uncle's absence could be felt physically.

It was then I saw him.

My heart leapt.

Aadhi was walking right towards me from inside the house. He had grown taller, and he wasn't a boy anymore. He was a handsome man, looking so serious, so focussed and so bearded that my mouth dropped open. There was a tinge of melancholy on his face that sent a shudder down my back, but I smiled at him. Dad hugged him.

"Didn't know you were here," he said.

Aadhi fell at dad's feet and sought his blessings. I checked out his physique as he bent down. He had turned broader and fitter. It seemed he had channelled all his pain into his body.

After getting up, he pulled me in for a gentle hug, his familiar scent adorning my nostrils, pulling the fond memories in an instant. I was caught in shock, but I gently patted his back and moved away, mostly because my dad was there, who didn't seem to mind. Probably, they were alright with this match, but I wasn't sure I was. We had grown apart.

But the moment I inhaled his scent, my eyes welled up, and I wished I was his as soon as possible.

A few hours passed by as Dad and Rudran uncle engaged in a serious discussion about Veera Explosives' petition in the high court. They were debating whether to let Advocate Madhav Kumar handle it. A boring topic. So, I whispered to Aadhi whether we could get out of there. As usual, he instantly agreed. We decided to drop by his, I mean, uncle Deva's house. Being there was painful. The air usually used to be heavy with the memories—the happier ones, and heavier now with death.

Aadhi offered me some snacks, and I ate them in silence.

"How are you?" I asked gently.

"Getting by."

I nodded.

"Same," I said.

"I missed you," he said blatantly. "A lot. But you drifted apart, and it was understandable. Things got too haphazard."

"I missed you too," I said, blinking away my tears. "Everything changed, is it?"

"Nothing did," he replied, and my heart raced. "I promised you, remember?"

"What do you mean?" I asked, holding back a smile.

"Exactly what you think. I still love you."

I broke into tears and laid my head on his shoulder. He caressed my head just like old times.

"I thought some other girl had landed you 'coz you have grown handsome," I said.

"Trust me, they tried."

"And what did you do?"

"I told them the truth."

"And that is?" I asked curiously.

"That I was in love with a girl who won't love me back."

I nodded. "That must have sent them on their way."

"Pretty much," he smiled, still caressing my head.

Silence.

"That's not true," I said.

"What isn't?"

"What you said. You're not in love with a girl who won't love you back," I spoke gently, holding his arm. His body stiffened for a second and I would have loved to see his expression. He lifted my chin up, and I smiled at him. He swallowed hard, his eyes turning wet. It was the most beautiful thing to watch.

Just when I decided to drown all my misery in one deep brush with his lips, the doorbell rang. I jumped and Aadhi patted my back, as if saying, 'Hold that thought. I'd be right back.'

He opened the door. I heard him say "Who is this?"

"Can I come in?" I heard a man speak. I got up and joined Aadhi at the door. Outside stood an extremely tall, bulky man with a face so mundane that I almost sighed. He looked like a bar bouncer to me—the bodyguard types.

I gazed down. There was a snake tattoo on his arm.

"Who are you?" I asked.

"Your uncle Deva knew me," he said.

The tone in which he said that made the ground beneath me shake. I looked at Aadhi. His face grew tighter and tighter.

"And you are?" he asked.

"My name," the man said and paused as if he had never once said his name to anyone else, "is Christopher."

30
SHOCK WAVES

He sat down, his mundane face now sad and scared. Aadhi gave him some water.

"She is on her way." He started. As if we knew who *she* was. She? My heart thudded. Was *she* the woman from the picture? The murderous nightmares came to mind. I brushed them away. We did not bother to ask who she was. We first had to know who *he* was.

"Who are you, sir?" Aadhi asked. "How did you know my father?"

"Is there anyone who doesn't know your dad?" he asked. The question seemed rhetorical, more than appreciative. We stayed silent. "I worked for Vijay."

Thunder jolts passed through me.

"Okay. What do you want with us?" Aadhi asked.

"I was his bodyguard. Anyhow, that's how others saw me."

His voice was strangely feminine—a stark contrast to his appearance.

"And what were you, really?" Aadhi asked.

"I was, well, his executor."

My spine tightened in horror.

"He asked me to do some bad things," Christopher spoke in his feminine voice. "Very bad. And I did it for him. Will you believe me if I say I'm not a bad man?" he let out a melancholic laugh.

"I don't know how I was born," he continued. "I don't know if my parents left me on the street or if I was born there. All I knew was that I ended up on the street. I used to be bigger than the other urchins who played with me. And one day, by mistake, I pushed a boy on a fence in anger. The rod got into his nape and he died. The other kids ran away, and I panicked. A man was passing by in his posh car. He came down and spoke to me. Told me everything will be fine if I came with him. I did. I had no choice. He gave me nice food, shelter, and a blanket. A blanket! Can you imagine? I had never once had the comfort of a blanket ever in my life. And the food? Oh my! It was an emperor's feast! Who could say no to that?"

He took a sip of water and then continued.

"I grew up in their home running errands, doing the chores for Jagan, Vijay's father. When his son grew up, I was asked to do the chores for him, to take care of him. He hated his dad's money. He wanted to make it on his own somehow, which made him into this ruthless being, cunning, jealous, self-absorbed and so vicious. He liked torturing people, liked exerting his power over them. Seeing them struggle gave him happiness."

"Then what happened?" Aadhi asked, as I figured he already knew this trait of Vijay.

"Before Veera Explosives came onto the scene, just like Deva, there were a few people who always had problems with him. And as I was the only one he trusted a lot, so he would ask me to…"

Aadhi's face grew pale.

"You said you were the executor," he said. "You were his hitman."

"Yes."

"You had no choice," I said. "You were stuck with them. They gave you this life, and you were asked to surrender."

"Like how Doctor Faustus surrendered his soul to Satan," he smiled forlornly.

"Tell me one thing," Aadhi said. "Did you kill my father?"

"I was coming to that."

"Just answer my goddamn question," the vein on his temple popped like a worm. "Did you or did you not kill my father?"

"Thing is," Christopher said in his feminine voice, his biceps flexing in tension. "I don't know. I might have."

* * *

Aadhi collapsed on the couch beside me.

"Thing is," he said, glaring at Christopher, the vein growing thicker and now twitching. "I don't know. I might have to kill you right now. I might have to bury your body in the fields."

"Aadhi, calm down," I held his arm. Though I felt his urge to push me away, he didn't.

Christopher held his head down as Aadhi glared at him, his body turning ice cold.

"Let's hear him out," I said. "Let's see what happened. This might be our only chance to know the truth."

Aadhi did not move, his eyes tearing up in anger. I looked at Christopher and he held his head down. Something told me that he would have an idea about the mysterious girl from the picture. A knot tightened in my stomach.

"Before I tell you what happened, you have to know about a girl," Christopher said.

The knot tightened to its maximum.

"Her name is Archana."

And the knot broke. I shut my eyes and chewed the insides of my cheek. Christopher started weeping, to my horror.

"Who is she, and what happened to her?" I managed to speak. "How is she connected with uncle Deva?"

The doorbell rang. Aadhi got up to open. A woman stepped in. She was wearing a modest kurti and a denim bottom. She was carrying a file in her hand.

"I'm Nikita Krishnan," she said. "I should be there when he speaks," she pointed to Christopher. "I'm an advocate from Coimbatore District Court."

"Are you his lawyer?" Aadhi asked.

"No," she paused to swallow. She seemed in her mid-thirties and she looked so sorted and strict in a way. "I'm Archana's lawyer," she said, and my pulse raced. "Though she couldn't be here today."

* * *

31
THE GIRL FROM THE PICTURE

We sat around at uncle Deva's dining table. I wiped it clean of the dust. He never used the table when he lived here. He preferred to sit down on the ground and eat, always mentioning that it digested the food better. His wife, however, preferred one from the antique store, and he had kept it as a souvenir after her passing.

"Archana was my friend," Nikitha started, her eyes sinking with each passing word. "She was one of a kind. Extremely intelligent. Prodigal, in fact. What I'm about to tell you happened after her graduation," she paused to swallow again. Every time she did so, I felt like doing the same. "She belonged here in Achipatti. Well, the truth is she didn't belong here. She was different. Too much for the village, for which she was judged badly. She left for Chennai for her studies."

"From our village? Any chance we know her?" Aadhi asked.

"She is the daughter of the Mannivannans."

My mind swirled. Where had I heard the name before?

Manivannan.

When I met uncle Deva for the first time, I had heard him and uncle Rudran talking about him—something about them going missing. Uncle's face was sullen during that conversation. My heart thudded. Are they the parents of the girl from the picture?

"Manivannan," Aadhi repeated, thoughtful. "I have heard dad talking about them."

"Something about them going missing," I spoke immediately.

"Yeah," she made that dry swallow again. "After a terrible incident that ripped them apart."

We stayed silent, none of us having the strength to ask what it was. Nikitha glanced at Christopher before starting to speak again. He had his shoulders slumped as if a rock was weighing him down.

"Ten years back she came to the village after her graduation. That's when she saw your father." She paused and her eyes darted as if she was about to say something mischievous.

"What?" I asked, though I kind of knew the answer.

"Well, she fell in love with him."

"What?" Aadhi squeaked in his baritone voice. "Wasn't she young?"

"Yeah."

No more words spoken. Aadhi could understand that his father attracted a lot of women unintentionally back in his days. He had that charm about him, and Aadhi wasn't blind to it.

"She wanted to help Deva with his pursuit against Veera Explosives. Out of love for him or out of genuine interest for the good, I'd never know."

"Oh I'm sure it was the love," Christopher said.

I looked at Aadhi curiously. He mirrored my face back at me. We were both wondering how Vijay's hitman would know this.

"It's wrong. I wonder how dad approved of this," Aadhi said.

"Of what? Her loving him? What's there to approve of? It's her wish. He did not reciprocate in any way."

"Not that… her helping dad with his dangerous pursuit," Aadhi said.

"Oh that," Nikitha squirmed. "He didn't allow that, either. He wanted to protect her. But you don't know how pushy and determined she could be."

"And she got into trouble because of this?" Aadhi asked.

A long pause. Nikitha again did that dry swallow. This time I really wondered if she had gobbled up a metal ball which was trying hard to find its way down. I pushed the glass of water to her. She downed the contents and then said something that confirmed my fears.

"She was murdered because of this."

32
THE UNTOLD STORY

Over the next two hours, Nikitha filled us in on the details—on what she had gathered from the things she picked up from her long conversations with Archana. Mostly about how deeply Archana cared for Deva and how ready she was to bring Veera Explosives down. Nikitha clearly decided to leave out the part about the intense physical attraction that Archana felt for him, though their phone conversations would mostly be about that.

Each spoken sentence sent slivers of lightning into our heart. Nikitha told us about the Gunasekaran video and how that must have urged Archana to meet him directly. She buried her face in her palms.

"I got an SOS message from her. And the plate of Gunasekaran's car."

A tear escaped her right eye.

"She told me Deva was on his way. So I managed to reach him and let him know that she was in danger. I don't know when he reached. I don't know what happened after that."

She threw an aching glance at Christopher, hoping he would be easy with his side of the story this time, unlike the way he was when she found him. Confused and scared, which made him utter every word the way it happened. She had heard the raw version—it had numbed her insides and made her succumb to nightmares for months on end, she had lost focus on work and had had innumerable appointments with the therapist. She wasn't ready to take it again.

Christopher started to talk.

Nikitha hoped he would be kind with his words.

She thought wrong.

He started off with how she *must* have been taken to Vijay's house in Kotagiri from Gunasekaran's place at Coimbatore North, where she *must* have been thrashed by Vijay. Christopher began describing everything just the way it had happened.

He spoke about how painstakingly Vijay raped her just because he thought her virginity shouldn't go to waste after her death. His comments about her body when he was raping her—everything was uttered by the executor in the most graphic and intricate way. Nikitha shut her ears and put her head on the table. I held on to Aadhi in fear as Christopher spoke. Aadhi put his arm around me, his eyes widening and his grip tightening with each passing word. When he described how she called him Anna and pointed to her ripped body, I broke into tears. He then told us about how he covered her naked, torn body with his shirt and carried her and ran to save her.

"I still can't forget it," Christopher said, wiping his tears. "The way she called me 'Anna'. No one has ever called me that. It did something to me. I felt a stinging ache of guilt. The way she trusted me, even when I was asked to kill her. The way she held onto me like a child the moment I lifted her off the ground."

He wept.

"Wait," Aadhi said, still glaring. "Why didn't you stop that bastard?" His voice was so low that it sounded like he growled.

"I…uh…"

"You're obviously bigger than that bastard. Stronger. You could have ripped his head out from his body in a jiffy. But you didn't. You stood and watched him devour her. Why? And now you're giving graphic details as if enjoying it. What the fuck is wrong with you?"

He hung his head low. The snake-tattoo on his arm moved as he twitched his arm in tension.

"And what took you so long to say this out loud? What took you ten frigging years? How do you sleep at night?"

"There is something you should know about me," he spoke. "I'm a weakling. I'm spineless. I'm a coward. I don't deserve to be called a man. That element was there when I was a kid. When I was free. When I was myself. I stood up against the wrong amidst my pears. That element died within me years back when I started working for Vijay. Every time I heeded to him and killed someone, a part of me would die along with them. Thing is, if I were a completely bad person like Vijay, I would have at least acquired less karma. But I'm a good person," he paused to weep. "And I let it all happen because I never once could stand up for what is right."

Aadhi's anger increased still. I knew from his face that he had a comeback for this, but I wanted to know what happened after that. So, before he could open his mouth, I spoke.

"Then what happened in the woods?"

"Uh," he shook himself to come to terms with the change of topic. "We heard footsteps as I was running. Before I could realize, I was hit from behind."

"Vijay was back?" Aadhi asked. "He found out you were trying to save her?"

"No, it was uncle Deva," I said with pride. "Must have been him."

Christopher nodded, his eyes tearing up.

"He thrashed me like he was about to kill me. He screamed like an animal. He swore at me in the most ruthless manner while he landed his punches in my face and gut."

"Why didn't you stop him?" I asked.

"He thought he deserved it," Aadhi spoke for him. He nodded.

"I did."

"Yes, you did," Aadhi said, and I held his arm to make him stop.

"Then Archana said something, and he went towards her. She told me I was trying to save her. He put her on his lap... and then," he said and Nikitha gently squeezed his stone-like palm from underneath the table. Maybe she didn't want us to know something. Maybe uncle Deva and Archana shared a moment before she died.

"What happened?" I asked, my eyes filled with tears. Aadhi held my arm tight.

"Vijay had hit her head on the ground so badly. She didn't stand a chance. She passed away in Deva's hands."

Silence.

"What did you do after that?" Aadhi asked.

"I lost my mind. My stability..."

"And?" He asked as he already knew the answer.

"I uh..."

"You ran." Aadhi said. "Yet again, away from the truth. Away from doing the right thing."

"Yes," Christopher said, shrinking physically with every word. "I ran."

"You left my dad alone with her torn up carcass and you ran."

"Yes."

"Aadhi," I said. "Don't."

"Literally," Aadhi smiled as his words choked up. "You said you're actually a good person, right?"

Christopher shrunk again, ready to take the blows.

"You're worse than Vijay. At least he was a bad person who did bad and stayed bad. Didn't pretend to be good. He was himself, the monster he was. But you," Aadhi paused, "your silence, your inability and your cowardice, in spite of being good and knowing better, made monsters like him thrive. You let him get away. You let the bad flourish. You blinded yourself to the sins he committed. You let the wrath survive.

Goodness in cowardly people like you is more dangerous than the wrath of monsters."

"You're right," Christopher said.

"What did uncle Deva do?" I asked.

"He didn't want to bring her back to the village," Nikitha said. "Everyone would know what had happened to her, and it was the last thing Deva wanted. He buried her alone, deep in the forest. He didn't come out of the forest for days. He just roamed around like a madman, unable to do anything. I tracked him down only to know that he was hatching a plan to kill Vijay. I talked him out of it. It took me two days to pursue him to come out of the woods. I asked him to be sensible. I promised to help him fight this legally. I didn't want him to throw his life away in the name of murdering Vijay. So, he waited patiently. Apart from her SOS message and the license plate, there was absolutely no proof. People like Vijay and Gunasekaran would easily crush a baseless case like this. And once crushed by them, we would never ever be able to reopen it. Our only hope was to track the man who saw all this, tried to save her and ran away—the only person who could nail Vijay."

She pointed to Christopher.

"Vijay was also trying to track me down," Christopher said. "Of course he figured it out. He was always irritated by the good in me."

"And he had more eyes than we ever could," Nikitha added.

"What about Archana's family?" I asked.

"I informed them of what had happened. Everything."

"Why? Why would you kill them like that? At least they would have thought their daughter had gone missing."

"No, Shravya," Nikitha said. "Hope is worse than pain. Pain is like a stab to the chest—painful, but a quick death. But hope is like inserting the dagger achingly slow into your heart, watching you wriggle with agony, watching the pain grow and spread, watching the force of death consuming you slowly, watching life slowly drain out of you. A quick, painful, drop-down death is much better than this. No matter how much the truth hurts, at the end, we crave only for that. The truth is always better. Always."

I nodded. I did not grasp the depth behind the words, but it sure made sense.

"They left the village. At first, they wanted to sue Vijay. But I told them they couldn't. They would lose their lives too, and the whole village would become a graveyard. I asked them to wait. But they left overnight, and I did not see it coming. They couldn't handle it."

"And you were looking for them?"

"Yes. Everyday Deva would physically go around and ask, village by village. He used to travel in search of them and help people on the way to distract himself from falling into a dark place. I kept looking for them in my ways. We still couldn't locate them. We were trying to locate Christopher, too. Thing is, nobody knew his name, what he did and where he was from. Everyone just knew that he worked for Vijay. His identity was kept a secret. No one called him by his name. Vijay had faked his identity easily. We couldn't locate him after he ran away. We had no place to start, let alone find him."

"Then?" Shravya asked.

"I came back," Christopher said. "I met Deva in the dead of the night two years back, while he was coming back to Achipatti. I apologized for leaving him alone that day. I fell at his feet and promised him I'd do the right thing."

"Did he beat you up for leaving him?" Aadhi asked.

"Not once," Christopher said. "He pulled me in for a hug."

Silence.

"That was your father," Christopher wiped his tears. "He understood I was scared. He never once blamed me for being a chicken. He even appreciated me for trying to do the right thing."

Tears welled in the eyes of everyone.

"He was a gem," Christopher concluded.

"I'm not like him," Aadhi said.

"I can see that."

Aadhi gave his death stare at Christopher.

"Not that I expect you to be," he said, his head hung low, shrinking again.

Aadhi became thoughtful as he nursed his pulsing head.

"What is it?" I asked.

"To think about it," he started. "My dad had no one to support him all his life. Throughout, he was alone. No one stood beside him in his toughest, his highest or lowest. Hell, he never had highs. All lows. All downs. All falls. Still, he protected everyone. He looked after everyone. But who looked after him? Even I left him alone when she was murdered. I left him. I wasn't happy with his way of life. I left him alone to suffer. Maybe if I had been supportive, he would have shared this incident with me. He was facing such a big trauma all alone. He was facing the guilt, the pain, the grief, the pressure—all alone! Who am I to blame you, sir? For chickening out. I was worse than you," Aadhi said and Christopher shook his head.

"He was proud of you," Christopher said. "The little time I spent with him, he always talked about you. About how you were mature for your age and how smart you were. I just knew one thing. He loved you more than anything else."

Aadhi's head spun and he couldn't stop his tears. I held on to him tightly and he pulled away. No amount of comfort could help him. He wished things were different. He wished he could once tell his father how much he loved him.

"What happened after that?" I asked, afraid that Aadhi might cry.

"I had given Deva a number of burner phones for him to contact me," Nikita said. "He informed me that Christopher was back, and that things were set for the court. He wanted me to find an unfindable place for his hideout, because we knew if Vijay found out, Christopher would be killed in no time. I gave him a place in a dilapidated godown in Coimbatore on the outskirts. Everything worked out just fine until," Nikitha paused.

"Vijay found out somehow," Shravya said.

"Yes, he did," Nikitha said. "I knew immediately that he had sent people on the lookout for Christopher. Well, he had asked them to kill him as soon as they saw him. No torture, no enjoying his pain, nothing. It was too late for revenge. He just wanted to silence Christopher, because if he opened his mouth, Vijay would be done for."

"So, what did you do?"

"We faked Christopher's death."

"How?"

"I'm a lawyer. I have contacts. Like pathologists who can help me access bodies."

"You used a dead body that looked like him?" Aadhi asked.

"Yes, I did. A big man who met his end through murder. He was stabbed to death. His face was mangled in the fight beyond identification. Some gang tiff. He had no one to claim his body, that poor man."

"And he looked just like him?" Shravya asked, pointing to Christopher.

"Yep. Same body."

"Oh my god! Don't tell me you used his body somehow," Aadhi said.

Nikitha swallowed again and shut her eyes.

"Yeah, we did. We took it to Kotagiri and placed it on the edge of the forest where Archana was murdered."

"And as Vijay was keenly on the lookout for me, the body wasn't difficult to find." Christopher said.

"Imagine his joy then!" I said.

"Hell, he threw parties for a week after that. He thought one of his men had murdered Christopher and even announced prize money of twenty-five lakhs for them," Nikitha said.

"Obviously one of them agreed."

"Yep."

"So, things were sorted. You guys were all set to rat Vijay out to the court," I said. "Then what went wrong?"

"Your uncle visited the collector's office, remember?" Christopher asked.

"Yeah sure. Things didn't go his way there."

"And he did something afterward," Christopher said.

Aadhi heaved a sigh of dismay, as if he could already guess what his father might have done. He was used to his impulsive deeds.

"He went to meet Vijay in his Kotagiri house," Christopher said and Aadhi mouthed 'fuck' and banged the table with his fist.

"He thrashed Vijay physically. They probably got into a row," Nikitha said. "And Vijay must have toyed with him, must have pushed him to the edge, saying that he could do nothing against him legally. And your father proved him wrong by uttering Christopher's name."

"No!" I screamed. "Fuck. No!!!"

"Don't tell me that's what got him murdered," Aadhi said, his eyes tearing up. "Please don't."

Nikitha nodded. She swallowed again, and this time I didn't want to push the bottle towards her. Aadhi and I stopped holding hands. Physical comfort works only if the grief is manageable, if it stays within the radar. If it goes beyond the limits, physical comfort is the worst thing one can face. Everything looks fake and irritable. We don't even feel our bodies then. Our senses shut down, and invoking our senses with a touch is the worst thing one can do. People holding on to each other at the peak of pain is overrated and dramatic. It happens only on screen. We prefer to be withdrawn and paralysed when it happens. Only when the pain becomes manageable, do we crave for physical comfort.

At that moment, Aadhi and I did not prefer to stay in the vicinity of each other. Aadhi held his head and walked out of the dining area. I didn't go after him. I couldn't. I was paralysed.

After about five minutes, Aadhi came back, his eyes red and his face blank. It was then that I reached out to him and he hugged me. Physical comfort worked.

"I'm sorry," Nikitha said. "But yeah. His impulsive behaviour got him killed. Vijay knew for sure that finding Christopher would be impossible. So, he did the one thing he had been putting off for so long—silencing Deva. He knew that Christopher, who chickened out once, would never have the guts to come back and rat him out."

"But he didn't know your role..." I said.

"Nope. That's the silver line in this grey cloud. He never found out that someone was helping Deva. Anyway, they manipulated Syed and lured Deva out to the hill and killed him. He silenced the only guy..."

"...with the loudest voice," Aadhi completed.

Nikitha nodded.

"But we are not ready to give up," she said.

"What do you mean?" asked Shravya.

"We are going to court."

"What do you mean you're going to the court?" asked Aadhi, his voice sharp. "What's the use now?"

"This is what your dad fought for. Archana lost her life over this stupid company. We've got to end this," said Nikitha. "Once and for all."

"And how do we do that?" I asked.

"This is insane," Aadhi said. "It was all a game for him in which he kept winning. What's the use of making him lose now?"

"He has to lose someday," Christopher spoke in his feminine voice, now rough with emotion, "and only I can do it."

"I know you *can* do it," said Aadhi. "The question is, *will* you do it?"

"Aadhi, stop!" I yelled. "Enough of picking on him. Enough! He's here to do the right thing. Give him some respect."

Aadhi turned quiet.

"They have filed a petition at the Coimbatore District Court asking them to drop the blast charges on them. Now is the time to strike," Nikitha said, not swallowing anymore. Her voice had turned crystal clear and sharper. She knew she could do it. Her over-confidence had always been her knight in shining armour.

"Strike unexpectedly," I said. "They'd think they have won. Oh, how much I wish I could lay my eyes on their terrified faces when Christopher walks up to the stand!"

"Why aren't they looking for Christopher anymore?" Aadhi said. "We are literally in dad's house. Even the slightest doubt that he could be here would ruin this entire plan."

"Like I said," Nikitha started. "He had the loudest scream silenced. Why worry about the tiny squeal?"

Literally and figuratively, she was right about the big man's voice, which made him chance a painful glance at her. This lightened the mood, but no one smiled.

"Will anyone help us in the court? Usually, the public prosecutor represents victims, right? Who's the prosecutor now?"

Nikitha gave off a proud, egotistical smile. The air of confidence and a tinge of assurance had me doubting if she was, in fact, the prosecutor.

"Is that you?" I asked.

"Nah," Nikitha let out a smile. "Someone better. Someone powerful. Someone righteous like your uncle, someone who knows not what fear is, someone that can't ever be bought with money, someone who has the loudest voice in the courtroom. Someone who wages war when asked to argue. Bottom line, someone thousand times better than me."

"Who is that?" she asked.

"It is Public Prosecutor Sathiya Moorthy," she smiled. "The only man who could turn a courthouse into a battleground!"

The air turned hotter with each passing moment. Hotter with assurance, as if extending physical comfort to the grieving room. Nikitha's tone and assurance filled the room with raw, unadulterated hope, and at the same time, with some doubt, too. We had been through enough. We were drained of all hope completely and even a tinge, well even a wave of hope from someone who had done a lot to help Deva uncle, felt scary. Though we knew all this had robbed us of an integral piece of our souls, we knew we had to try—one final attempt, one final swing with all we have.

For uncle Deva.

33
THE BATTLEGROUND

20 October 2019

Two days after their arrival, Nikitha had arranged a meeting for us with A. Sathiya Moorthy, the prosecutor, in his office in the Coimbatore District Court. We had reached Coimbatore by bus. Nikitha and Christopher travelled by a car with a fake license plate and black sun films on the windows hiding the big man.

The wind blew in my face as I rested my head on Aadhi's manly shoulder. Everything seemed to be happening so fast that we barely talked about the weird incidents and the weirder stories that we had been exposed to in the past two days. Aadhi, as usual, gave me the window seat and held my hand. I looked out at the passing clouds, the squealing school kids, the raging screeches of vehicles, the peaceful passers-by, but nothing entered my mind. I looked at everything but I did not *see*. I wondered how the public prosecutor will be. Would he live up to Nikitha's words? Or was she exaggerating? I had to find out the hard way.

"Aadhi," I said, holding on to him.

"This is our last try," Aadhi said, as if he foresaw my question. "Let's give our best and see what happens."

I nodded.

In half an hour, we were at the Coimbatore District Court. I wondered how many times uncle Deva would have climbed up and down the stairs of courts like these, with grit, with hope, with confidence. And now, his soul was dependent on newbies like me and Aadhi. My eyes welled up.

We should somehow do something to honour him. We should at least try to help him achieve what he fought for so long.

A car screeched to a halt near us; a car with windows darker than dusk. We knew in an instant it was Nikitha. She beckoned us to follow her inside the court, and so we did. The court was massive. The red and white facade sent tingles down my back. The reason courts were built with so much magnificence and massiveness, I think, was to somehow give us hope. Would we trust the court to sort out our issues had it been a four by four cubicle or even a hall for that matter?

Nope.

After we were at a safe distance from the outside world—the main road, I mean—Christopher was allowed to step out of the car. Nikitha wore a cream-coloured sensible kurti and a patiala pant. She looked majestic. The kind that people would immediately trust to sort their issues. No wonder she was a successful lawyer. However, in the past few years, she had lost the air of confidence, the authority, the urge to nail it in the court, showing the guilty ones who the boss was. She had always been looking over her shoulder, turned a tad docile, and stopped believing in herself as much as before. Her over confidence had turned into just a mediocre amount of confidence that any junior lawyer might have.

I remembered the number of times she swallowed and how she was on the verge of tears when she was speaking about Archana. How it would have been for her to have lost her friend? I don't know if she considered her a friend, but I was sure Archana was someone Nikitha admired and cared about.

She was fighting battles she didn't have to. Nikitha led us to an office that had an ancient, worn-out blue board with bold white paint that had turned dirty with time.

A. Sathiya Moorthy
Public Prosecutor

We entered, and I immediately felt the emptiness of the room. The walls were plain, the floor clean, the windows curtainless, with a plain table in the middle and behind it sat an elderly man.

I took a step back at the sight of him. You remember the feeling when you walk inside the principal's office? This was worse. The very sight of the man made me feel guilty of the mistakes I never made. He had that effect. He seemed angry and was the type that looked into the souls of people. I wondered if he could just *see* to it that the guilty ones confessed. He was a tall, big man, wore an advocate's black robe, was dark complexioned, with salt and pepper hair, and with so many flaws on his face that there was nothing plain on his face. Maybe that's why he kept his surroundings plain, to counter the effect.

He nodded at Nikitha.

She went and sat opposite him on the chair and introduced us. He barely looked at us and nodded while I almost bowed. Christopher stood near the door, hanging his head low, and the prosecutor barely looked at him.

"The petition hearing is today, sir," Nikitha said.

"Who's our lawyer?" he asked, and his voice was the exact opposite of Christopher. It was so deep that I felt the floor shake beneath my feet.

"It's Madhav Kumar," Nikitha said, adjusting for the umpteenth time in her seat. She was clearly intimidated by him and had the utmost respect for him. As he was acknowledging only her in the room, it was obvious that he respected her, too.

"Madhav Kumar's good," he nodded and flipped through the case file Nikitha submitted with much aggression. "But I have got to do it right."

Somehow that sentence made me assured that he really was going to do it right.

"Sir, we also found out that Veera Explosives in Achipatti was built on squatter land." Nikitha said.

"Good," he nodded again. "This keeps getting better."

"This is Madhav Kumar sir's report," she handed over another file. "On the squatter land thing."

"And his file on the death of Deva is on the way."

"Good. That's not for today. That should be the climax. That's the final nail for their crucifixion."

The office door flung open. A young man who looked like a junior lawyer entered.

"Sir, the three owners of Veera Explosives have arrived. And," he paused, "they are with their lawyer."

He hung his head down.

"Who?" the prosecutor barked, his base voice now baser with curiosity.

"It's uh ..." the junior hesitated, "Pasupathi."

I did not know who that was, but both Nikitha and the prosecutor's face grew pale, their eyes bulging out. They looked at each other and grew paler still. I knew from their reaction that he was someone huge, a badass. I just did not know how much.

"The hearing is in an hour," the junior informed and left. "Judge Heera Devendran will be here in some time."

* * *

"Why did you look scared when the lawyer mentioned Pasupathi?" Aadhi asked Nikitha as we sat down in a canteen nearby. Nikitha wanted to grab her first meal of the day before the war, as she called it.

"Pasupathi is one of the best criminal lawyers in the history of Coimbatore District Court. You know how many cases he has won? Every goddamn case ever! He has had zero defeats. Every lawyer who has stood against him has faced torture and trauma before the D day. He is a badass! He will go to any extent to win. He doesn't care about ethics. Cares only about victory. He pulls up dirt even on the judge to blackmail them into turning the case his way."

"Sounds like bad news!" Aadhi said.

Nikitha munched her sandwich and Christopher stuck with just tea and vada. Nikitha was urging him to eat well, for he was the prize of the day. He kept refraining. Probably the adrenaline had shot up. I hoped he wouldn't run away again.

"Don't run away!" Aadhi said, and I squeezed his arm in shock. Christopher gave him a pained look. "This is your final chance to do the right thing. Final and only chance. Don't mess this up, please. For my father. For the naked, torn- up girl who trusted you in her final moments. If you mess this up, I promise on my father that you will never be able to forgive yourself. You're so much stronger than you think you are. Please don't give up."

Aadhi held back his tears, but Nikitha couldn't. She broke into tears. I knew in that instant the intensity of agony she had been holding back. She dropped the sandwich on the plate and wept like a child.

Christopher took the sandwich and shoved it gently in her palm.

"I won't run," he said, swallowing down a lump. "Trust me."

* * *

Aadhi and I sat at the back of the courtroom. Naturally, my parents and Rudran uncle's family should have been here, but they had lost all hope when uncle Deva had passed away. It was just the way with elders. They had too many responsibilities; too many other pains that they tend to just stop fighting after a point of time. Nothing to blame. Maybe that's why Nikitha had decided to reach us to rather than the elders. We were more inquisitive, and well, jobless, to take this seriously.

The clerk announced the entry of Judge Heera and asked us to stand.

"You may be seated," she said after reaching for her chair.

Judge Heera Devendran. She was a golden lawyer back in her days and rose to this position due to her ethical and intelligent ways. Basically, she was a good person.

A few minutes later, in walked Vijay, Gunasekaran and Ramachandran in their best clothes and wearing smug looks on their faces. My heart thudded, and I felt my blood hum. I imagined how they must have stabbed my uncle to death on the hills. I closed my eyes and prayed. I prayed to God that we should somehow win. They were followed by a short, white-faced puny man with no flesh but just bones, which again seemed flexible and punier than his skin. He wore glasses that barely stood on his face. I wondered if he would just collapse on the floor like a pack of cards.

"He is Pasupathi," Aadhi said and showed me google images on his smartphone.

"Really? This guy?" I asked. "Did Nikitha exaggerate?"

"No. She actually told pretty much the gist. This guy is savage. Don't judge a book by its cover."

The prosecutor and Nikitha entered the court. And then entered Madhav Kumar. This was all so weird and dramatic—like a scene from a movie. There were only a handful of people apart from us in the courtroom. Mostly people from Veera Explosives. Only me and Aadhi were the people against Veera Explosives.

The courtroom was simple—a small hall with the blindfolded lady justice holding the balance. The clerk spoke.

"Your honour, this is the case of the petition of Veera Explosives owners to free them from the charges of the blast in the village of Achipatti."

"I, the Public Prosecutor, represent the defendant—Achipatti village." Sathiya Moorthy got up and said, and the courtroom murmured.

"I, the plaintiff," Pasupathi got up and spoke, and I was taken aback. His voice was deeper than the prosecutor's and he spoke with so much grit and confidence that the entire court stopped murmuring, "represent the petitioner Veera Explosives." He sat back down with a smile that sent a shiver down my back. His confidence seemed out-of-place due to his appearance.

"She didn't exaggerate," I whispered to Aadhi, "I can feel the chills."

Aadhi shushed me.

Sathiya Moorthy got up towering over Pasupathi, and faced the judge.

"Your honour, if you've forgotten the brutality of the blast, let me remind you. The Veera Explosives factory was built in Achipatti without the permission of the people."

"Objection," Pasupathi got up and said it with a smirk. "Irrelevant."

"Your honour, let me paint the whole picture."

"I'll allow it," she said and Pasupathi sat back down with a grunt.

"Our man here, Ramachandran," he went towards him, "stepped into the village saying he intended to grow a plantation and bought the land. Then they started the construction of this explosives company. How clean."

"Objection!" Pasupathi got up.

"Sustained. Get to the point, Mr Sathiya Moorthy."

I wondered if he was actually good. I chanced a glance at Nikitha's face. She looked more confident than ever, with a permanent smile. Maybe this was the prosecutor's way of starting. To distract the court with unimportant details and urge a lot of objections, make everyone think he was losing, so that when he swivelled in the right direction, they'd be gobsmacked and the fireworks would begin.

"Over twenty-five people were blasted to a pulp on 1 December 2016. Even now, we do not know the actual number because certain bodies were not claimed. This happened due to the utter negligence of Veera Explosives. The people of Achipatti and several surrounding villages conducted rallies asking them to shut down the factory.

Nothing happened. The factory is still running, and there has been no technological advancement to increase the safety. Now, petitioning to do away with this case is the damnest thing. The system should be punishing them for this, let alone thinking about letting them go."

Vijay's face tightened.

"Objection." Pasupathi groaned.

"Agreed," Sathiya Moorthy said. "Let me be kind with my words."

His voice was so full of sarcasm that I let out a chuckle. "Your honour," he turned to the judge. "I urge you to re-look at the cruelty of the owners of Veera Explosives. They absolutely didn't care about the people who worked for them. They just cared about the money, which made them go low on safety. They have spent about ten crores on the equipment." He submitted a file to the clerk, who passed it on to the judge. "And just three lakhs on the safety equipment. They have completely flouted the safety protocol. This was just a formality to them."

The judge nodded and scribbled something down on the paper.

The prosecutor sat down and Pasupathi got up. I held my breath.

"Your honour," he said as he got up. His steps were filled with so much confidence—a lot more than the prosecutor. "Veera Explosives is a very reputed company dating back to the nineties, started by four business magnates ..."

"Objection." Sathiya Moorthy sighed as if urging Pasupathi to stop the ass-kissing.

"Sustained. You too, get to the point Pasupathi," the judge said. The more I viewed the proceedings, the more I realized that the judge was the actual badass.

"Alright, alright," Pasupathi shrugged, as if the entire court was stupid. "Anyway, what happened was a mere accident. Accidents like this happen in every industry all the time."

"Objection, your honour."

"Proceed."

"The price of this accident was more than twenty-five lives blasted beyond identification."

"What do you say to that, Pasupathi?" the judge asked.

"It is highly unfortunate, yes. Our deepest condolences to the families of the victims. But Vijay has done everything in his power to help the people of the village. He was the largest employer. He was held by the police and the CBI for days."

"Objection, your honour."

"Proceed."

"It was all just an eyewash. The charge sheet was not filed for ninety days and he came out without any consequences."

"It was the mistake of the system, not Vijay. You cannot blame my client for the mistake of the police," Pasupathi's voice vibrated.

"You really think the system did it on its own without any monetary help from your client?" Sathiya Moorthy smirked.

"Your honour!" Pasupathi complained.

"Sathiya Moorthy!" the judge gave a warning look. I'm sure the judge and the prosecutor had a dynamic.

"I'm sorry, your honour. But you should note this point."

"Where's the proof that my client bribed the police?" Pasupathi asked. "Can you produce it?"

"As if the proof exists for under-the-table exchanges," Sathiya Moorthy smirked. I couldn't help but smile, but the judge made him sit back down and allowed Pasupathi to continue. He went on and on about how Vijay had always been kind to the people and helped them a lot after the 'unfortunate' incident.

"If they had lost their trust in Vijay," Pasupathi made his million-dollar point. "Why would they still work in the factory in hundreds?" He submitted a file to the clerk. "These are pictures and proof that the people still work for Veera Explosives. The same people who created a scene during the blast in the name of a rally are seen working at

Veera Explosives now. How do you explain that?" He glared at Sathiya Moorthy. Their eyes met. But the prosecutor had nothing to say. We all knew this would be the point they would target. The one thing uncle Deva would never forgive.

Silence.

"What happened was an unfortunate accident and I urge you to release Veera Explosives from the blast charges. They are the largest supplier to the Indian Army. They are known for selling the explosives at a very low price to the government. We should actually join our hands and help companies like these instead of targeting them. They are actually helping to protect the nation. The charges should be dropped so that they can continue helping the people without a stale stain on their name. That's all your honour."

The judge began scribbling.

Pasupathi and the entire team were all smiles. Some even shook hands, thinking that they had actually won the case.

"Your honour," the prosecutor started. "With your permission, may I call upon someone who worked for Vijay?"

My breath stopped. Vijay's face grew pale.

"Objection. Irrelevant." Pasupathi yelled in his bass voice.

The judge looked at the prosecutor.

"Your honour, this person is the key witness to a crime and this would turn the entire perspective of the hearing."

"Objection."

"Overruled. I'll allow it," the judge said. "You can bring them in."

The court held its breath. I grabbed Aadhi' hand. I offered prayers in my head that Christopher should walk in. To be frank, I was still afraid he would run away. I shut my eyes tight.

I heard the court's murmur increase in pitch and I opened my eyes. Christopher stood in the witness stand, his face the most confident I had ever seen. Tears rolled out of my eyes. Aadhi leaned in and said, "This is it."

Years of seeing things go only downhill suddenly turned, and we had no idea how to react. I looked at Aadhi. His eyes were filled with tears, and his face was the happiest I'd seen since his father's death.

* * *

Though Vijay was in the front row on the right side, I could catch a glimpse of his face when he turned around. When Christopher climbed up on the stand, I guess he ran out of words and was paralysed. I craned my neck to look at his face. In a second, he turned back to look at us. His face was extremely pale, and it looked like he was having difficulty breathing. He locked his gaze with Aadhi and they looked at each other.

"Proceed," Judge Heera said.

The prosecutor headed to the witness stand, kept his palm on the railing, held eye contact with Christopher, and spoke.

"Could you please tell the court your name?"

"I'm Christopher."

It was then that Vijay turned back and looked at the proceedings. I felt chills the entire time he held eye contact with Aadhi.

"Sucker," Aadhi said, and I shushed him.

"What do you do, Christopher?" Sathiya Moorthy asked.

"Right now, nothing."

"Interesting. What were you doing before?"

"Objection. Irrelevant!" Pasupathi yelled and his confident voice did not seem that way anymore. I shifted in my seat, my blood humming in happiness.

"Relevant only." The prosecutor said. "Wait and watch."

Damn.

"I'll allow it," Judge Heera said. "Proceed."

I had a feeling she was more interested in seeing how things were going to turn out.

"Answer me, Mr Christopher," the prosecutor said, "what were you doing before you were not doing anything?"

"I was working for Vijay Kumar."

"In Veera Explosives you mean?"

"No."

"Then?"

"I worked for him. As his ... uh ..."

I held my breath.

"You can say it. Come on," the prosecutor said.

"Objection!" Pasupathi screamed. The base tone was long gone. "Persuasive."

"Overruled. Go on Sathiya Moorthy."

I almost slapped my thigh with joy. The judge was the queen here.

"I was his executor," Christopher said after a deep sigh.

"Did I hear that right?" the prosecutor cupped his ear dramatically. "Care to explain the meaning of the word?"

"I used to do *things* for him."

"You mean to *execute* things for him?"

"Objection!"

"Overruled. Go on."

"Yes," Christopher said. "I executed things for him. Sometimes even people."

Silence in the court. Even Pasupathi was too stunned to speak.

"Let me get that straight, Mr Christopher. Are you confessing in front of our honourable judge that you have killed people for Veera Explosives' owner, Vijay Kumar?"

"That's right," Christopher said.

"Can I hear you say it?"

"Objection. Asked and answered," Pasupathi just wouldn't let go.

"Overruled."

"I confess that I have killed people for Veera Explosives' owner, Vijay Kumar."

Even Sathiya Moorthy was taken aback for a second. Christopher had become stronger than ever. It was too pleasant and majestic a sight to watch.

"And have you ever worked for anyone else who was in contact with the owner?"

"Yes," Christopher answered quickly before Pasupathi threw an objection card.

"Anybody we know?"

"Yes," Christopher took a deep breath. "Minister Kalingaraj. I have killed once for him."

Shock waves spread throughout the courtroom.

"You mean Vijay's wife's father's brother and the Health Minister, Kalingaraj?"

"Yes."

"You mean the same health minister who gave loads and loads of compensation to Achipatti people."

"Objection. Asked and answered."

There it went.

"Sustained." Judge Heera made frantic notes. She was getting more interested. "Proceed with further questions, Sathiya Moorthy."

"I just have one question, your honour," the prosecutor said, heaving a sigh. "Mr Christopher, do you know anyone called Archana?"

This was the moment Christopher was waiting for. Before he replied, he played Archana's last moments in the forest like a video in his mind. A teardrop escaped his eye. Pasupathi didn't care to object. He knew the judge was obviously not on his side. He needed some time and discussion with Vijay before he could give a daring comeback. He waited.

Christopher darted his eyes to fixate it on Vijay's face before he could answer. Gave a little smile as if asking, "What can you do now, you son of a bitch?"

"Yes sir!" Christopher answered, wiping his tears, "I know her very well."

The court time was over and the hearing was adjourned to three days later.

34
THE D-DAY

Earlier today
Coimbatore District Court

The hearing had been adjourned to three days later, which was today. Pasupathi had asked for some time from the judge to build up some dirt; to play his master card. The Archana episode, which had come out suddenly, had caught him off guard. Probably he needed the time to ask Vijay to come clean about Archana, whoever she was, so that he would get a better picture of the incident.

I'm sure Vijay wouldn't have hidden the truth from his lawyer. I was sure he was paying him in millions only because he knew about his crimes. I was very sure he was going to pull some dirt up on Christopher. Probably the unintentional murder he committed when he was a kid.

After lighting the lamp on the hill, I was back at the court, holding on to the little hope I had. Aadhi was standing in front of the table, his hands folded.

"Let's see," the prosecutor said. "We have one final blow that would bury them."

"What's that, sir?" Aadhi asked.

The prosecutor looked at him. "It's your father."

I kept the file on the table. Advocate Madhav Kumar—uncle Deva's brother-in-law—had given me the file yesterday, the moment it was ready, for my pooja on the hill—the mini Pachaimalai.

"This is it?" the prosecutor asked.

"This is it," Madhav Kumar said. "The complete file on Deva's murder."

"Got anything worthwhile in it?"

"See for yourself," Madhav Kumar said with a pained smile. He then beckoned us to leave. We left the prosecutor alone with the files as he drowned himself in the only truth that would change our lives forever.

* * *

The court was back in session. When Judge Heera stepped inside the hall, it felt like a familiar whoosh of warm air had blown through the rows of seats, calming the pulsating hearts of those who were waiting with hope.

"Please be seated," she said, and we obliged. Christopher was called back to the stand. He seemed way better today; not as confident as before, but calmer and more comfortable. It was better because the fire in him was gone. The urge to destroy Vijay, the guilt for having made a mistake—everything was gone. He was better prepared to face the day today. Without pressure, with just responsibility—the only time we operate at our best.

The Veera Explosives clan arrived. They seemed fresh, well-rested, and I felt an unfamiliar thud in my heart. Did they find something that will ruin us?

"So, Mr Christopher," said Sathiya Moorthy. "Let's speak about Archana, shall we?"

He passed a small file to the clerk, and he passed it to the judge.

"Yes, sir," Christopher said. His feminine voice was now pleasant to hear.

"Archana was a law graduate from Achipatti—the first person from the village to graduate from college. When she came back to the village after graduation, she decided to collect evidence against Veera Explosives, as that was the time the construction was going on. When this came to the company's notice, they circulated a fake video so that it reached her. Your honour, with your permission, I want to play the video in the honourable court."

"Proceed."

The objection king probably had decided to play it quiet today. It scared me more.

The clerk played the video on the giant screen on the right side of the judge's table. Gunashekaran hitting Vijay and Vijay falling down on the ground. The court was taken aback in shock after a collective 'ooh' after the punch. They were quiet for a good long minute and then the murmuring started, with all of them craning their necks to see Gunashekaran and Vijay. Vijay's face tightened in shock. I saw his jaws go slack.

"Objection, your honour. What's the proof that the video isn't fabricated?"

I sighed.

"Sustained."

"We know it's not fabricated," the prosecutor said smugly. "Or even if it is, how do you explain this?" He passed what looked like a bill to the clerk. "The IP address from which the video was first circulated is consistent with the IP address of Vijay's house."

The court held its breath. I wondered how the prosecutor laid his hands on stuff like this. Wow!

"So, it was planned," he said.

"Objection. It could have been anyone's foul play. Can't blame my client for that."

"Fair enough. Let me tell you what happened after that. Archana was somehow exposed to the video. So, instead of taking anyone's help, she decided to confront Gunashekaran by going to his house in Coimbatore North. Thing is, she never returned after that."

He waited for an objection, but nothing came.

"Mr Christopher," he looked at him, "care to tell us what happened?"

My heart thudded.

Over the next half an hour, Christopher repeated everything that he had told us in uncle Deva's house. My heart thudded as each of his words sent wave-like lightning in my nerves, yet again. The entire court listened with their jaws slack, a deafening silence breaking through. Vijay did not move. He seemed paralysed with his head held down. I wondered if he had passed out. I wished he had. I shifted in my seat, not uncomfortably, but rising higher and higher with each sentence of Christopher's, maybe due to the satisfaction or pride or the fact that the truth was out there without any external force halting it. This was the first time the world was coming to know the truth about Vijay—the one thing my uncle had struggled to do throughout his life.

Christopher wept during his monologue, but made no effort to hold it back. The judge's eyes widened at times and she, as usual, took frantic notes. But when he reached the part where Archana had called him Anna and pointed to her body, she held her face in her palms, throwing her pen away.

I held Aadhi's hand tight as Christopher finally mentioned how he had run away, leaving uncle Deva in the forest with her. Nikitha was called to the stand and spoke at times when it was needed, like the time when she received the SOS message and how she conveyed it to Deva.

Frankly, it couldn't have gone better. The session went just too well and our success seemed just around the corner. My mind was darting back to the time I had spent with uncle Deva—our swimming sessions, the nights when he drank and spoke his heart out, the times on the hill, the field—and finally seeing him wrapped in a dull white cloth. We were doing this for him and it was working out in the end.

Something told me that this was him working all this out from above, not us. I started weeping and Aadhi pulled my head to rest on his shoulder.

Sathiya Moorthy made sure every word saw the light of day, and hence he made sure Christopher did not leave out any detail by throwing gory questions at him about the rape. His questions shocked the court, but we all knew it was needed to make sure every soul in the hall hatred Vijay with their guts. When he was satisfied with the effects, he sat down.

"That's all, your honour."

"If I may ask Mr Christopher a few questions," said Pasupathi, adjusting his big specs on his flimsy nose. He stood up and walked over to the stand.

"Yes, sir," Christopher said.

"May I ask how you came in contact with Vijay Kumar's family?"

Christopher stayed silent.

"Let me tell you how," Pasupathi said. "You accidentally or intentionally murdered your little friend, didn't you? Another orphan like you. You pushed him on the fence and he died. Yes or no, Mr Christopher?"

After a long pause, Christopher let out a meek yes.

"You would have been in the juvenile prison forever. Mr Vijay Kumar's father, Mr Jagan Kumar, took you in with him due to concern and protected you. Hell, he adopted you as his child. Isn't that right?"

"Yes."

"Objection, your honour." Sathiya Moorthy roared. "It was all just a safe game. To bring a scared little kid into their home, provide him with the pleasures of life, show him heaven and then manipulate him to do their dirty work for them."

Silence in the court.

"Sustained. How do you explain that Pasupathi?"

"Christopher murdered a lot of people after his first killing." Pasupathi groaned deeper. Nikitha was right. This sure seemed like a battleground.

"Objection. He was just following Vijay's and his father's orders," Sathiya Moorthy said.

"Sure," Pasupathi came towards Sathiya Moorthy and looked deep in his eyes. "Prove it."

Silence.

"I don't want to get into the details," he turned around to look at the judge. "But science says that the person who got away with the first murder is very likely to kill again. I say that Christopher committed the other murders and used the power of the family to hide these murders and finally, when the chance came, he turned against them."

"My honour, really, that's the stupidest thing I've ever heard!" Sathiya Moorthy said.

"Mr Sathiya Moorthy!" the judge gave a warning look.

"Hard facts mostly sound stupid," Pasupathi said.

"What about Archana then?" Christopher asked. "I saw it with my own eyes."

"But you never stopped them, did you?" Pasupathi said. "If you are a real man which you claim you are right now, inaudibly by criminalizing Vijay, why didn't you stop Vijay? Or even kill him during the course? I'm sure the system would go easy on a man who killed someone to stop a rape! Why didn't you do that?"

Christopher stayed silent, his eyes growing wet and his limbs stiffening.

"I was weak!" Christopher shouted, banging the railing. "I was fucking weak! I let her suffer, and I watched it, though I wanted to grab this bastard by his throat and bang his head on the trunk of a tree. I wanted to twist his erect penis and pull it out of his body. I wanted to smash his face with my bare fist until it became unrecognizable. But I couldn't do it. I badly want to do it now, but I don't want to ruin my only shot at bringing justice to that girl. So yeah, lawyer! I didn't respond because I was weak. As to your other question, about the science bullshit, kindly check if all the guys I murdered had a beef with me or with Vijay.

You don't have to dig too deep. It is available on the news. They were all other Devas."

Pasupathi became too stunned to speak after Christopher's unfiltered monologue that couldn't have been more real.

"Your honour," Sathiya Moorthy started, "about Deva's death."

"Objection. Unrelated," Pasupathi roared.

"Totally related."

"Overruled," the judge nodded at Sathiya Moorthy, asking him to proceed.

"This is the autopsy report." He passed a file to the clerk, and he passed it to the judge. "Without his executor, Mr Christopher, present, probably Vijay had decided to take the job up himself. Because his hair strands were found on the crime scene."

Deafening silence.

"The pathologist confirmed it. The hair strand contains his DNA."

This was the final sixer. Madhav Kumar had made it happen. He had worked on the Deva murder case and he had somehow made the truth see the light of day.

"Objection. It could have been from any time when Vijay travelled up the hills," Pasupathi said.

"That's the thing," Sathiya Moorthy smiled. "Vijay has never ever travelled up that hill. We have the villagers from Achipatti, who live around the factory and around the hill. Let's have a chitchat with them."

All of them said in chorus that they had never seen Vijay leave the factory when he came to Achipatti, and the ones near the hill said that they had never seen Vijay climb up the hill.

"A man as powerful as this would definitely move around with his bodyguards. The villagers would not have missed the sight of him if he climbed up during the day. So, if his hair strand is unusually found on the hill, that too near Deva's body, I wonder how it happened."

He then proceeded to go on about Syed's phone call, the burners and how Syed was never seen again.

Pasupathi's throat was dry. He was engaging in deep discussion with his team, urging them to speak up, but all the owners had gone paralysed.

"The factory is built on squatter land, and here's the proof," Sathiya Moorthy was on a roll. He handed over the last file to the clerk.

The judge read it and scribbled on her papers.

"I urge you, your honour," Sathiya Moorthy said, "to kindly give the highest punishment of death penalty to Vijay for the murder of the workers in the factory and for the innumerable murders executed through his executor Christopher, for the rape and murder of Archana and finally for the brutal murder of the one man who battled for his village, Deva."

He took a pause and then said, "I also urge you to immediately seal the Veera Explosives factory in Achipatti village, for it has polluted the entire village and is built on squatter land by illegally extorting it from the villagers."

* * *

We now wait for the judgement. It is scheduled for three days later, and we wait patiently. We know for sure that the case is one-sided—entirely leaning on our side. But if Vijay buys out the judge, it would be impossible for us to win. We wait patiently. Sathiya Moorthy and Pasupathi have a number of meetings with the judge before the final day. I wonder if there are some buy-ins. My parents, Rudran uncle and the entire family are present for the judgement. They had a lot of questions and doubts regarding how we brought the case to the court's notice so efficiently, but they are more than happy that it somehow happened. Me and Aadhi won't be grounded, I hope.

The judge enters after the clerk's announcement. Vijay and the clan enter after a few minutes. There is no confidence on Vijay's face—no smug look, no sarcastic smile, no 'I'm the shit' face. He looks pale but at peace, as if he is ready to accept what comes his way. He better do.

"The defendant is guilty of all the said charges," Judge Heera says and I almost squeal in happiness. "The court sentences Gunashekaran and Ramachandran to a twenty-year jail sentence and life imprisonment for Vijay Kumar."

We break into hugs and tears find their way out of our worn-out eyes effortlessly. Aadhi runs to Christopher and climbs on top of him for a bear hug. Christopher almost crushes him in happiness. Nikitha hugs me for a good two long minutes. Rudran uncle is in tears and my dad collapses in the chair, unable to process the emotions. It is all done and dusted. Though the death penalty for Vijay is off the table, it didn't matter to us. His dying was useless. It would have been a release, and he doesn't deserve it.

He should rot in jail thinking about what all he did and how he could have done things differently. Life imprisonment is always worse than death. Death, I feel, is the most humane punishment one gets out of a court.

Aadhi comes towards me and looks at me, his eyes wet. He smiles through his tears.

"I love you," he says and hugs me.

"I love you too."

We know our family is watching us, but we don't care. Somehow, they don't stop us. I think it is too evident that we are together. There isn't a better match for me and my parents know it.

"Do you think he loved her?" I ask Aadhi.

"Who?" he pulls away and looks into my eyes.

"Uncle Deva. Archana. I feel Christopher and Nikitha aren't telling us something. It is true that Archana loved uncle Deva. It's obvious. But," I pause, "did he love her back?"

Silence. Something tells me that he did.

"I don't know," Aadhi says, thoughtful. "But I know one thing for sure. He honoured her."

I nod and smile through my tears. He hugs me again.

Vijay is cuffed and is taken out of the court.

* * *

Someone lurks behind a tree with a knife in his hand. He is wearing tattered clothes and his once-upon-a-time handsome face is now caked with mud. The moment he sees Vijay, he lashes out. He launches at him with uncontrolled fury.

Vijay looks at him and his eyes bulge in shock. Before he or anyone can react, the knife plunges deep into his heart, knocking the man's breath and life.

"This is for bhai," he says as Vijay collapses on the ground, his eyes still bulging out.

A loud commotion and squeals bring us out of the courtroom.

I see Vijay down on the ground with a knife plunged in his chest, his eyes wide open and a man who looked like a Neanderthal being held by the police roughly for the murder.

His face looks familiar. My eyes widen. He looks at me and smiles. The same handsome face that was seen near uncle Deva all the time.

Syed hasn't aged at all.